"What Are You Going To Do?"

"Give you something to hate me for. I'll get the truth out of you no matter what I have to do."

"I've never lied to you," she insisted, knowing that all he wanted was to kiss her, slide his hands down her back and line her body to his.

And then he was doing just that. She felt his desire; the heat of his hunger for her seeped through her clothes and found a reciprocal flame.

DOROTHY VERNON

is an author well known to all Silhouette readers. An avid reader herself, as well as an accomplished writer, she is particularly fond of lively heroines who live in her own native British Isles.

Dear Reader;

SILHOUETTE DESIRE is an exciting new line of contemporary romances from Silhouette Books. During the past year, many Silhouette readers have written in telling us what other types of stories they'd like to read from Silhouette, and we've kept these comments and suggestions in mind in developing SILHOUETTE DESIRE.

DESIREs feature all of the elements you like to see in a romance, plus a more sensual, provocative story. So if you want to experience all the excitement, passion and joy of falling in love, then SILHOUETTE DESIRE is for you.

I hope you enjoy this book and all the wonderful stories to come from SILHOUETTE DESIRE. I'd appreciate any thoughts you'd like to share with us on new SILHOUETTE DESIRE, and I invite you to write to us at the address below:

Jane Nicholls
Silhouette Books
PO Box 177
Dunton Green
Sevenoaks
Kent
TN13 2YE

DOROTHY VERNON
Sweet Bondage

Silhouette Desire

Published by Silhouette Books

Copyright © 1982 by Dorothy Vernon

First printing 1983

British Library C.I.P.

Vernon, Dorothy
  Sweet bondage.—(Silhouette desire)
  I. Title
  823'.914[F]   PR6072.E75

  ISBN 0 340 32926 2

Printed and bound in Great Britain for
Hodder and Stoughton Paperbacks, a
division of Hodder and Stoughton Ltd.,
Mill Road, Dunton Green, Sevenoaks,
Kent (Editorial Office : 47 Bedford
Square, London, WC1 3DP) by
Richard Clay (The Chaucer Press) Ltd.,
Bungay, Suffolk

Sweet Bondage

1

When Gemma bought the handbag at the church jumble sale, she had no idea it would figure in a chain of events that was going to land her in deep trouble. If the handbag hadn't been pointed out to her she wouldn't even have seen it. She had popped into the church hall on her way home from work, not to look at the jumble, but in the hope that the cake and produce stall would supply something tempting for her supper. The good ladies of Ash-le-dale were all worthy cooks who liked to show off their versatility as well as their skill. And so the obligatory assortment of Yorkshire parkin, scones, and cakes was complemented by mouth-watering pizzas and savory pies.

It had been exceptionally busy at the library where Gemma worked. She'd had to skip lunch to do some cataloging which Miss Davies, her superior, had thrown at her, apologizing that it should have been completed days ago but had slipped her mind. Gemma's stomach had started to grumble around four o'clock, but not one word of complaint had passed her lips. She liked Miss Davies and didn't mind putting in the extra effort to get her out of a fix. It meant, though, that she was ravenous now, but too weary to think of preparing anything satisfying to eat, thus her hope that the cake and produce stall would solve her problem.

Her luck was in. Although there was very little left she spotted just one, probably the last of a batch, of Mrs. Topliss's famous Cottage Pies. It was in an oval earthenware dish, which was returnable, and Gemma knew from past experience that a delectable mixture of minced beef, onions, ketchup, and herbs lay beneath the mashed potato topping. She handed over the money and was happily carrying her trophy away when she heard her name called. Turning her head she saw a hand waving for her to come over.

"Gemma, I've been trying to keep this hidden all day on the off chance that you'd pop in. I couldn't imagine anyone else having it but you. What do you think?"

It was a clutch bag in soft, luxurious leather, dove-gray in color, the same shade as Gemma's eyes. But it wasn't that which said that it was tailor-made for her.

"Look, it's got your initials on it. G.C. Gemma Coleridge."

They both knew that the monogram on this hand-made clutch bag, which came from a prohibitively expensive shop in Knightsbridge and which could be Gemma's for a donation, had originally stood for Glenda Channing. Glenda was Gemma's age, twenty-two. As they were both petite and shared the same fair coloring they bore a passing resemblance to one another. But after that, all similarity ended.

Glenda was the adored and pampered only child of

estranged parents. She had chosen to live with her father, Clifford Channing, the property tycoon. Her mother lived in the south of France. Home for Glenda was "The Hall," as the large Edwardian house on the outskirts of Ash-le-dale, a beauty spot in the Yorkshire Dales, was known locally. The table she sat at glittered with fine crystal and candelabra; the food she ate was prepared by a French chef and served to her by servants. She received a generous allowance from her father and had charge accounts in all the top stores. The freedom of the world was hers, and she made good use of it, always jetting off somewhere. The exotic places that Gemma could only hope to read about in the travel section of the library were commonplace to her.

Gemma was an orphan. She lived alone in a cottage at the end of the village, a low, stone-built dwelling with tiny windows jutting deep into the solid walls. The plumbing was temperamental, the kitchen range ancient, and sometimes, especially when the snowdrifts crept up the door, she was lonely. Church jumble-sale days excepted, she cooked her own meals, which she ate at the kitchen table, and she paid her own bills. She held her head high and was proud of being beholden to no one.

She looked at the clutch bag with pensive longing, because it was an exquisite thing, but before she could open her own handbag to take out the money to pay for it she had to fight down an uprising of fierce pride that rebelled at taking someone else's cast-offs. She was never certain afterward why she bought it. Was it because she hoped that by having it in her possession some of Glenda's glamorous lifestyle might rub off onto her? Or because her neighbor was so pleased to have saved it for her and she was too tender-hearted to disappoint her by saying she didn't want it?

Having bought it she abandoned it on the back seat of her old red Mini, giving the Cottage Pie front seat priority where she could keep an eye on it. Running the car was expensive, but it was a necessary extravagance, providing her with a means of transport between the village where she lived and the market town of Ashford, where she worked and did most of her shopping. The bus service linking the two points was atrocious, only operating on the even hours, and there was talk of even that service being axed.

Things carried on as normal for the next two weeks. She went to work and came home, driving her Mini through the superb scenery of the dales, small in compass, but magnificent in detail, with the narrow road curving in and out between the folds of the hills. Houses were dotted like pearls among the skeletal winter trees and the limestone crags provided a dramatic backcloth.

When she married Barry Holt, if she married Barry, and the if was getting bigger every day, she would have to move to town because village life didn't appeal to him. Not that there had been any talk of marriage between them, or even of an engagement, but in these parts when a man "walked out" with a woman on a regular basis it was understood that the eventual outcome would be a walk down the aisle.

She woke up one sparkling, frosty morning to the knowledge that it was Thursday and she didn't have to see Barry for two whole days. The fact that she was pleased about this gave cause for thought. A further bonus was that it was her day off. The past few days had been even more frustrating than usual and it was a treat not to reach for her workaday tweed skirt and library smock, and instead feel the soft fullness of a dress in lavender-colored wool round her narrow hips and the anticipation of a morning's shopping and browsing.

She breakfasted on toast, marmalade, and coffee, washed the dishes, and put them away, and slid her arms into her warm sheepskin-lined jacket. On a last-minute impulse she transferred the contents of her everyday handbag into the gray clutch bag she'd bought at the jumble sale and locked up her little cottage in a cheerful mood.

She stowed her boots in the car, because she could drive better in her shoes, and set off, maintaining a pace suitable to the road. It occurred to her that if circumstances did take her away she would miss this switchback ride along the narrow road boxed in on either side by parallel, and apparently never-ending, drystone walls.

She glanced into her driving mirror and was perturbed to see Glenda Channing's white Lincoln Continental coming up behind her at speed. She intended to pass her, of course. It was all right for Glenda. A scraped wing wouldn't give her household budget the jitters. Gemma's own foot went down on the accelerator, keeping her eyes peeled for a good place to pull over. Being forced to the side in this overbearing, inconsiderate way was no unusual occurrence and as she pulled onto a grass verge she was fuming. Glenda Channing thought she owned the road. Not only that, she didn't even have the courtesy to acknowledge Gemma's courtesy in giving way as she passed and sped on her way.

Gemma arrived at Ashford still feeling indignant. As it wasn't a market day she easily found parking in the square and made for the shops, looking at the frivolities, unserviceable satin mules and French perfume in cut-glass bottles, but buying necessities, three very functional yellow dusters and a scrubbing brush. The groceries she intended taking back with her had still to be purchased as she paused at Betty's Cafe. It was run on Victorian lines, cakes displayed on tiered cake stands, fine china and silverware, and an atmosphere of genteel, bygone elegance. Luxury never comes cheap and Gemma only meant to peep in at the bow-fronted window and then do what she normally did, walk on. But this once, something, she would never know what, made her open the door and walk in.

Perhaps it was something to do with her unsatisfactorily drifting relationship with Barry, or her pique at being forced to the side of the road by the quiet elegance of Glenda's custom-built car, but she felt strangely restive and self-critical. Surely it was up to her to choose the direction of her life, not sit back listlessly and accept what she was being given.

As it was between times the morning coffee rush had dwindled off and the lunch-time crowd wasn't yet congregating, so she had her pick of the tables. She chose one by the window with a nice view of everything going on. She gave her order to the waitress and sat back in patient expectation. The waitresses seemed to be taking advantage of the lull to grab their own tea break. An idle glance out of the window showed her Glenda Channing walking by. Glenda seemed to check her step as she caught sight of Gemma, and then she came into the cafe. This didn't surprise Gemma because it was the sort of place that Glenda would patronize; what did surprise her was the purposeful way Glenda strode to her table and asked if she might share.

Gemma was too taken aback to say anything but "Of course." She waved a hand in the direction of the other chair. "Help yourself, Miss Channing."

Could it be that Glenda was feeling ashamed of her earlier lack of consideration? If so, how amazing, but what had brought about the change of attitude? On the previous occasions when their paths had crossed Gemma had tried to be friendly but had always been given the big freeze.

"Call me Glenda," the other girl said, forcing a somewhat pained smile to her lips. "We are, after all, neighbors. I've been feeling for some time that we should get acquainted. Admittedly, I could have picked my time better. I'm afraid I'm not in a very good mood."

Gemma hardly needed to be told that. There was a petulance about Glenda's pretty features that was unattractive and her doll-blue eyes were dull and sulky.

It was Barry who had once likened Glenda to a doll. He had meant it as a compliment, because he ogled Glenda in rapt fascination whenever she came into view, but Gemma thought that if someone had said that about her she wouldn't have been flattered. And if she were a man she wouldn't be attracted by a china facade. The face to draw her eyes might not be as blatantly beautiful, but it would shine with intelligence and warmth and humor, and because it was a very human face the eyes would give out storm warnings when the occasion arose, but the mouth would never develop the pout of a spoiled child. She was unaware of this, but she could have been describing herself.

Suddenly Glenda thrust her chin forward and declared, "I envy you, Gemma. Your life is so uncomplicated."

What a stupid remark! It brought things that had been simmering all morning to a fast boil.

Before she could stop herself Gemma replied in heated retaliation, "What do you know about my life?" What did Glenda know about stamping library books all day and smoothing out difficult subscribers and battling cheerfully to keep ahead of the bills? Glenda wouldn't look at satin mules and French perfume and buy yellow dusters and a scrubbing brush! What did she know of feeling trapped, of serving a sentence of sameness, of getting up and making breakfast for herself and washing the dishes and clearing them away, and then going to work and coming home and preparing supper and washing the dishes and clearing them away all over again? Or of seeing Barry on Mondays, Wednesdays, and Saturdays with routine regularity? Glaring at Glenda she said, "Substitute boring for uncomplicated and you'd be nearer the mark."

"I didn't mean anything," Glenda said quickly, biting her lower lip. She added crossly, "I'd rather be bored than in the mess I'm in."

I'm sure Daddy will get you out of it. Contrition quickly followed the thought. Perhaps Glenda was in real trouble. She was certainly the type to attract it.

"I'm sorry, I shouldn't have let fly at you. Is there anything I can do to help?" It was not in her nature to shout at someone because she was feeling let down by life and too inadequate to do anything about it. Regretting her outburst, she said, "Why don't you talk about it? It might help."

"What could you do?" The contempt in Glenda's tone didn't match the speculation in her eyes, which had been there from the moment she'd caught sight of Gemma sitting in the cafe and been prompted to come in and join her.

"I could listen," Gemma suggested, ignorant of what was in the other girl's mind.

Glenda's chin lowered. Her expression turned guarded in a way that was almost furtive. "It's all been talked out, and everything has been decided very sensibly and rationally—but not by me. I suppose I'll take the course I've been told I must take, but that's not the point. It should be *my* decision. Don't you agree?"

"Oh, yes, most definitely," Gemma said, though with no idea what she was agreeing to.

Glenda's chin lifted and a smile of self-indulgence came to her mouth. "Thank you. I knew that you would be on my side."

"Hang on a minute. I'm not taking sides. How can I when I don't know what it's all about?"

"And I know that you would help me if you could," Glenda continued as if Gemma hadn't spoken.

"If I could, yes," Gemma admitted lamely, "but I don't see—"

"I've got to get away—away from them *both*. What's the good of escaping from the clutches of a domineering father to fall under the influence of someone who shows all the signs of being even more domineering still? I refuse to be bullied into doing something I might regret later. I've got to think this out for myself."

"Well—good for you," Gemma applauded.

What did one say in such circumstances? Even if she didn't know what was going on she agreed with Glenda's verdict of having the right to decide her own destiny. Hadn't her own thoughts just run a similar course and arrived at this same conclusion?

Changing the subject, Glenda said, "My car was making a funny noise when I drove into town this morning."

Gemma bit back the unsympathetic retort that it had sounded all right to her when Glenda had attempted to run her off the road and let her finish what she was saying.

"I've taken it to the garage that does Daddy's cars, but—and it's a terrible nuisance—they're so jammed that they can't look at it for at least an hour and I need transport *now*."

Gemma would have thought that the Channing account was too valuable for Glenda not to snap her fingers and get instant service. Her eyebrows lifted speculatively.

The implied question was ignored as Glenda's doll-blue eyes widened in appeal. "I wouldn't ask if the situation wasn't desperate, but . . . No," she said, her lashes sweeping down in a gesture that conveyed despair and touched Gemma's heart, "it's not fair of me." She sighed. "I can't ask."

Gemma would have been very dull indeed not to know what she was getting at. Without hesitation she opened her bag, ironically the same clutch bag which had originally belonged to Glenda, took out her car keys and placed them on the table. "If it isn't too much of a come-down and you really do need transport that badly, my car is parked in the square. You're welcome to borrow it."

Glenda's mouth lifted in triumphant laughter. "Do you mean it?" And then, before Gemma could have second thoughts, "Thanks so much, you don't know what this means to me." To which she added the unexpected rider, because a daughter of Clifford Channing had not been brought up to think of anyone but herself, "How will you get home?"

"Don't worry about me. I'll catch the bus."

Again there was something not quite genuine in Glenda's smile. "No, I've a better idea. Why don't you collect my car for me—if you're up to it?"

That ominously thrown taunt was no doubt meant to pay Gemma back for suggesting it would be a come-down for Glenda to drive the Mini and, if she were frank about this, she wasn't up to driving Glenda's car. It was as if Fate had been listening to her petty grumbles about the dullness and lack of purpose in her life and had said, "Right, this girl needs to be taught a lesson." It had thrown down the gauntlet and there was nothing Gemma could do but pick it up—pick up Glenda's car for her from the garage and accept the challenge.

"If you trust me with it, I'll collect it with pleasure," she announced.

"Splendid!" Glenda said, sealing the bargain. "Meridith's look after Daddy's cars, as you probably know. The mechanic said he'd leave it in the forecourt when it was ready. Here—you'll need the keys." She placed them on the table. "Why the look of surprise?"

"Oh . . . nothing really. I just thought the keys would have been left with the mechanic. I always have to leave my keys when I take my Mini in for service. I suppose they've got spares for yours?"

"Er . . . yes, that's it. The garage keeps spares."

"How shall we change back? Would you like me to come round to The Hall this evening to effect the swap?"

"Yes, do that." A smile played about Glenda's mouth. "Come in time for cocktails, *if you can make it,*" she added softly.

"I've nothing else arranged," Gemma said in acceptance. Cocktails at The Hall! That was one for the book. "Thank you, I'll look forward to it."

"Good." A waitress, who had apparently just spotted Glenda, came hurrying forward to take her order. Glenda forestalled her by standing up. "Now that I've got wheels I don't think I'll bother with coffee after all. The service here is getting dreadful. See you later," she called over her shoulder as she walked out, a smug, self-satisfied look on her face.

Gemma was unable to give the generous slice of gateau she had ordered with her coffee the concentration it deserved as she thought about what to wear for 'cocktails at The Hall.' The soft pink that suited her milk and roses complexion? Or would the dramatic blue that tended to drown her delicate coloring but made the most of her figure be better? And all the while something about Glenda's manner puzzled her, the mysterious smile on her lips, the way her words seemed to have a double meaning, and her gratitude for the loan of Gemma's car when it would have been so easy for her to call a taxi.

It wasn't until she went for her bag to pay her bill and her fingers closed round unfamiliar black patent leather that she realized Glenda had taken the wrong handbag. She could see how it had happened. Glenda must have forgotten discarding the dove-gray clutch bag. She had seen it on the table, a familiar possession, and picked it up without thinking.

Gemma felt guilty at having to dip into Glenda's purse to pay for her coffee and cake, but there was no alternative. She would have to recompense Glenda later.

On leaving the cafe she made straight for the square, hoping to catch Glenda before she got away and exchange handbags, but her red Mini wasn't there. She'd tried; there was nothing more she could do except wait until she saw Glenda this evening when she returned the car. She shoved the matter of the handbags to the back of her mind and enjoyed her browsing. A lack of money and her own disinclination to make free with Glenda's stopped her from buying the intended groceries.

When she judged that sufficient time had elapsed she made her way to Meridith's garage. The white Lincoln Continental was parked in the forecourt, just as Glenda had said it would be. The shoes she would have preferred to drive in were in her Mini. She looked down at her boots, wondering whether to take them off and drive in her stockinged feet, but decided against it. She'd see how it went. She unlocked the car door, settled herself in and, rather nervous and unsure of herself, drove off.

The mechanic had done his stuff because the engine wasn't making any funny noises now but was singing as sweetly as a bird. At first she was frightened that she wouldn't be able to gauge the car's unfamiliar width and length and hung back rather than take the risk of overtaking. But a strange thing happened. Sitting behind the wheel of such a lovely vehicle gave her confidence, or perhaps some of Glenda's panache had rubbed off onto her, because she began to enjoy the new experience. She almost didn't take the Ashle-dale road, toying with the idea of first going for a drive round, but thought better of it. She was a punctilious soul and she hadn't asked Glenda's permission.

Rounding a bend she saw a stationary car just a little way ahead. It wasn't a car she recognized as belonging to anyone local. It was dark blue in color, long, with classic lines, and like Glenda's car it was geared for speed but stuck on a road more suitable for the slow pace of a farm tractor. For the unwary these bends could be tricky and Gemma's first thought was that it had come round too fast and spun out of control. She was relieved to see no sign of damage to indicate that it had crashed into anything. It must simply have broken down. She would have stopped in any case at this obvious sign of trouble even if she hadn't been obliged to do so because it was parked in a way that left her insufficient room to pass.

She wound down her window with the idea of

calling out and asking if help was wanted and saw that the driver of the car was coming toward her.

The sight of the car had stirred her curiosity; its owner aroused her interest. He was certainly worthy of being looked at. He wasn't handsome in a picture postcard way, but bold-handsome, with a shock of black hair crowning a well-shaped head and slightly forbidding features. A nose that could be described as aquiline, a strong mouth, a granite chin. A somewhat somber face with eyes to match which appeared black from a distance, but as he got nearer she saw they were an unusual shade of olive. He was tall, a giant of a man combining broad shoulders and muscular strength yet having the lean physique of someone who keeps trim with a healthy diet and regular exercise.

He presented an awesome figure as he came striding toward her. Her pulse started to race in automatic reaction to the magnificence of him, or was it something to do with the way he came at her that made her feel—odd choice of thought, but—menaced?

"Run the car onto the grass verge," he instructed without preamble.

He spoke in an educated voice with just the trace of a Scottish accent. He looked normal enough, but you could never tell and she decided that it might be wise to humor him.

"Now why should I want to do that?" she inquired in her most pleasant conversational tone.

"For safety's sake, obviously. To leave it where it is would be asking for an accident."

"But I'm not leaving it here."

"No?"

"No!" This was getting to be ridiculous. Even men as divinely, spectacularly handsome as he was could not go round ordering people about, defenseless females at that, in this bombastic manner. "I'm not in

the mood for games. I don't know what this is all about
and I don't have the time to spare to find out. So
would you be kind enough to move *your* car to the
side of the road and give me room to pass?"

"You don't know what it's all about, do you?" he
scoffed. "Well, I'm very much afraid that I do."
Without more ado he reached through the window
and released the catch to open her door.

"I demand to know what you think you're doing."
She gasped, giving full vent to her fury at this outrage.

"Move over. I'll drive it onto the verge. Even if
you're irresponsible enough to leave it where it is, I'm
not."

"Now look here—" For all his dark-faced Highland
laird appearance, she wasn't going to stand for his
battling warrior tactics. "Just what do you think
you're—"

"Move! Unless you want me to sit on you and crush
you."

He looked as if he would. She wriggled onto the
other seat, more furious than frightened. He started
up the engine and drove the car onto the verge where
it wouldn't constitute a hazard.

"Now that that's safely out of the way and no
unsuspecting motorist is likely to run into it, are you
coming with me voluntarily or do I have to take you by
force?"

Suddenly it hit her. It was an abduction plot. A
laugh that had its origins in hysteria rose in her throat.
A kidnapper with a moral conscience, ensuring that no
one got hurt! She hoped his consideration would be
extended to her.

But why should he want to kidnap her? What would
be the profit? There wouldn't be any. Oh dear! Her
brain must be on the blink not to have realized this
immediately. He thinks I'm Glenda, she thought wild-

ly. He must think she was Glenda Channing because there would be no gain in kidnapping Gemma Coleridge, who didn't have one rich relative in the world to fly to her assistance. But Glenda Channing was a different proposition altogether. He would be able to demand a big ransom for her.

She must not panic. All she had to do was explain things to him and everything would be all right.

"You've made a mistake," she said in as steady a voice as she could muster. "I realize you think I'm Glenda Channing, because I'm driving her car, but I'm not. My name is Gemma Coleridge."

His head swiveled round and down to fix on her face. His eyes narrowed as he considered. "I've never met the girl, admittedly, but you fit the overall description. Early twenties, tiny little thing, blond hair, a face that's easy on the eye, and a figure that's hard on the blood pressure—masculine viewpoint, of course."

"Of course!"

"The first four fit. Can't tell about the other while you're hiding in that bulky coat."

"I'm not about to take it off," she said, hugging her sheepskin more firmly to her. "Any number of girls would fit that description. I am not Glenda Channing."

"Then why are you driving her car?"

"That's easily explained. Miss Channing took it into the garage this morning because the engine was making a funny noise. I offered to lend her my car to get her out of a fix. She needed transport urgently and I was in no particular hurry to get home. I said I'd collect her car and drive it home for her. It's as simple as that."

An explosion of laughter burst from his throat, the unpleasant sort that grated. "You must think I'm simple if you think for one moment that I'm going to swallow that."

His hand came forward. She shrank back in her seat, an automatic reaction that he acknowledged by the contempt that flickered in his eyes.

"I was only reaching for this," he said as his hand closed round Glenda's black patent leather handbag. "We'll soon see who you are, won't we?"

He opened it up. A few seconds' rummaging brought a twisted smile to his lips. "You lie with charming conviction and such a convincing innocence that you almost had me believing you. But I don't think I need look further than your driving license and credit cards for proof of your identity, do I, Miss Channing?"

Her eyes had closed in despair when she saw what he was doing. "I can explain that, too. The mix-up occurred in the cafe, Betty's Cafe, where I bumped into Glenda Channing. We shared a table. She left before I did and she took my clutch bag by mistake instead of her own handbag." Even to her own ears it sounded a lame story.

"That, Miss Channing, is straining credibility just a bit too much. I'd even go as far as to say that it is an insult to my intelligence."

"It's the truth," she said wearily, with little hope of convincing him. Everyone knows that a handbag is as personal to a woman as a wallet is to a man. Had the situation been reversed she would have been hard put to believe him. Yet there *was* a logical explanation and she must have another stab at getting through to him. "In normal circumstances I don't suppose she would have picked up the wrong handbag, but mine used to belong to her. I bought it at a church jumble sale."

"I'm not buying it. The lie, I mean. You've wasted

enough time. Are you coming under your own steam or do we wrestle?"

"We wrestle every inch of the way," she said, gritting her teeth. "I am not Glenda Channing and I am not coming with you."

She tried to sit fast. She made a spirited attempt, but she had about as much chance of resisting him as a feather has of knocking down a brick wall. He picked her up as though she was weightless, held her captive while he meticulously locked Glenda's car, and then ruthlessly tossed the car keys into the scrub beyond the drystone wall. "Unlocked cars tempt joy-riders. There's too much under that bonnet. Wouldn't like it on my conscience if some young hothead ended up wrapped round a telephone pole."

His conscience again! This was incredible. Even as she kicked and screamed and struggled and bit, all the while hoping in vain that someone would come along and rescue her from what seemed to be her inevitable fate, she couldn't help but see the comic side. Kidnapping ranked as one of the vilest of crimes. How could anyone who dealt in that kind of human suffering have principles? Something didn't make sense.

"I think you might be less of a distraction in the back," he said, bundling her into his car. "In any case, you'll be more comfortable. We've a long drive ahead of us and if you want to catnap you can. I brought a blanket to make you cozier. Don't try anything stupid, like attempting to jump out or hitting me over the head with your handbag or any other foolish trick. At the speed I intend to travel you wouldn't live to regret it."

"I won't, then, because I want to live. I want to live for the pleasure of seeing your face when you find out you've kidnapped the wrong girl."

"Not that again. Repetition is so boring."

"I said *when* you find out, as you will when you

discover that no one is particularly bothered about my disappearance. I've given up trying to convince you—for the moment."

Conversation temporarily ceased as the car's powerful engine burst into life and it shot off at hair-raising speed. He hadn't been joking when he said he intended to travel at a fast pace. It didn't take her long to realize that he was more than a merely competent driver. The car seemed almost an extension of his own hands, following orders from a brain that was like lightning when it came to anticipating road conditions. His skill gave her a sense of security.

She must be as mad as he was. Here she was being kidnapped by a dark-visaged speed-demon and she was thinking in terms of security! She ought to be sitting on the edge of her seat, biting her fingernails and shivering in terror. Why didn't she feel afraid? She felt a lot of things, anger, frustration and—yes!—a sneaking admiration for the magnificent way he handled the car and a rising sense of adventure, but no fear. Now why was that?

Chewing on that thought it came to her that he was no ordinary run-of-the-mill kidnapper. Not that she had ever met a kidnapper before; she had no yardstick to measure one by, but he seemed not only too kind but too affluent. On the other hand, she supposed that kidnapping could be quite a lucrative business. If he made his living by it, and providing he didn't make today's mistake too often and pick up the wrong victim, he could afford to dress well and run an expensive car.

Somehow, though, she thought this had the flavor of a one-off job, rather than a regular occurrence. If that were so, then her first, hastily reached conclusion that she was being abducted for money might also need revising. She could be wrong, but perhaps

Glenda hadn't been chosen solely on the grounds of her father's vast wealth. What if money didn't enter into it and she had been abducted to settle a score?

She'd heard enough village gossip to know that this was more than likely. Clifford Channing hadn't got where he was today without making enemies. He was reputed to have a nose for profit, seeing possibilities others missed, playing his hunches with boldness, flair, and ruthlessness, using people, then destroying them. It was said that he didn't care what hardship he caused and turned a deaf ear to appeals. It didn't matter to him if he left a man's life in ruins or broke a woman's heart. He liked female companionship almost as much as he liked making money. His lady of the moment was always "the one," but the cosseting never lasted. He quickly tired of her and she got the same shabby treatment he handed out to his business associates.

They had traveled for quite some time now, through daylight and into darkness. Funny how courage wanes when light fades. Things always seem more terrifying in the dark. She wished she hadn't remembered Clifford Channing's reputation. It wasn't funny anymore. She realized that she had been foolhardy not to appreciate the gravity of her position sooner, not that she could have done much about it.

"You're very quiet," he tossed at her over his shoulder. "Are you all right?"

"I'm a bit stiff. I could do with stretching my legs. And I'm hungry." And *scared*. She didn't add this, thinking it was better to keep her new-found fear to herself.

Perhaps fear wasn't something she could hide very well, because he said, "There's food in the car. I'll pull off the road as soon as I see a likely place. Oh, and you don't have to sound so frightened. You must know that I'm not going to harm you."

"Thank you," she said gruffly, comforted by the assurance despite herself.

The car headlights picked up a road sign indicating a lay-by ahead. He reduced speed in preparation and pulled in.

He flicked on the interior light, hauled out a food hamper, and lifted it on to the passenger seat by his side.

Opening it he apologized, "Only sandwiches, I'm afraid. But you do have a choice. Chicken or ham?"

"Chicken, please. I'd appreciate a drink of something first. Traveling long distances always gives me a thirst."

"Coffee coming up."

He took a flask from the hamper and unscrewed the top even before she said, "Lovely, thank you."

It was more than lovely. It was delicious. Hot and strong, easing a passage in her throat, dispelling the dryness and a little of the fear as well. The situation seemed slightly less menacing now that she was on the receiving end of human kindness in the form of food and drink. She wondered if he would be more disposed to listen to her now. She could but try.

"Honestly, I'm not Glenda Channing. There's no point in your kidnapping me. It was true what I said about collecting Miss Channing's car for her and the mix-up over the handbags."

"Still keeping up the pretense, are you? Anyway, who's been kidnapped? This was at your instigation; you've come voluntarily."

"You know that I've done no such thing."

"It's too late for a change of mind. I've gone to a lot of trouble to fetch you. Elaborate plans have been made." He swallowed the rest of his coffee in a gulp, put the cup back in the hamper and twisted round, his arms bent at the elbows and splayed along the back of his seat, granite chin resting on linked fingers to look at her. "I expected you to look more hard-boiled. Who would have thought that anyone with such an appealing little face could be so heartless and insensitive? I don't mind admitting that I'm having problems on that score. I've got to keep reminding myself of what you have done—and what you would do, given half the chance. You stand for everything I most despise. This time you've met your match. Clever as you are, you may as well get it into your head to drop the pretense because it isn't going to do you any good. I am not taken in, nor am I likely to be. Is that clear?"

"No, it isn't. I've landed myself in some bizarre situations in my time, but I've never been involved in anything like this before. I'm beginning to feel really angry."

His words had caught her on the raw. She wasn't used to being viewed so harshly. She liked to think that she was regarded kindly and admired for her caring and the way she concerned herself for others. She didn't think it was too conceited of her to know that this was the majority opinion and that most people thought well of her. Miss Davies, her superior at work, had once confided that she loaded things on her quite shamefully because she was a kind-hearted girl who never grumbled when asked for help.

It came to her that she was taking this personally, as if his biting contempt was directed against her and not the girl he thought she was, Glenda Channing. It also occurred to her that she was being paid back for her earlier dissatisfaction with a vengeance. Never again would she covet anyone else's lot as she had Glenda Channing's. Not only was this a severe punishment, but it brought a complete reversal of thought. She was glad she wasn't the other girl. She couldn't have borne it if he'd looked at her like this and known all the while who she was. Hard on the heels of that thought came a tremendous sense of self-betrayal. Why should she want him to think well of her? His code of behavior was hardly commendable, no matter what injustice, real or imaginary, had been done to him. She was a fool to want his good opinion.

"Hurry up with your coffee. You can eat as we go along. We still have a fair amount of ground to cover."

She had no option but to do as she was told. The fleeting idea of getting out of the car and making a run for it was squashed. It would be a waste of energy. He would catch up with her and bring her back. She was better hanging on and watching out for an opportunity that gave her a sporting chance of making an escape.

"Is there any point in my asking where we are and where we're heading for?" she inquired, thinking the information might come in useful.

He shrugged. "Won't do you much good to know, but I'll tell you. We're in the Border Country. Our destination is an island off the coast of Scotland."

"And . . . then what?"

She had already deduced that Scotland was his homeland. Although his accent was modified, possibly by an education received elsewhere, the rolling of the r's was a dead giveaway that he had links there.

His eyes moved with slow and purposeful precision down the slender length of her body, which was still obscured by the bulk of her sheepskin coat, and that strange bitter smile she had seen before touched his mouth once again. "We'll just sit it out and wait."

"Wait for what?"

"Until it's too late."

"Too late for what?" When he didn't answer she said, "Why won't you believe that I'm not Glenda Channing and I don't know what you are talking about?"

His voice was cool. "Of course you don't. You're sweet and innocent, as pure in mind and body as virgin snow. Still, time will disclose all, don't you agree?"

"Yes," she said, but without conviction.

She didn't like the way the net of circumstances had drawn her in. She didn't like the unexpected turn the conversation had taken. It confirmed her suspicion that she wasn't being abducted for money and had been snatched to settle a score. But it destroyed the assumption that the score to be settled was against Glenda Channing's father. It seemed that it was against Glenda herself.

Glenda's guardian angel had worked overtime on her behalf in planting her in Glenda's place. Lucky for Glenda, not so lucky for her. Her guardian angel had apparently taken the day off.

2

It was ironic that she had always wanted to go up into the Scottish Highlands, but for one reason or another she had never got farther north than Edinburgh. As a schoolgirl she had been held in thrall by Scotland's romantic and turbulent past. She had thrilled to the exploits of Bonnie Prince Charlie and Flora MacDonald and shivered to the gory tales of bloody battles and the ruthless butchery that took place as the Scots feuded among themselves or fought the invader in defense of their kingdom.

She had always known that one day she would come to this land wreathed in mist and legend, but she had imagined herself doing so as a carefree tourist in the bonny season of spring when the colors are young and fresh. Or the autumn, which is said to be the best time to visit Scotland, when the tinctures deepen, the purple becomes more dramatic and the oranges,

browns, and reds burn across the horizon. She hadn't
thought to come here on a dank and dismal day in
winter, the prisoner of a man who looked to the last
proud inch of him as dour and forbidding as the
fiercest Highland chief who had ever plagued and
terrorized his unlucky enemies.

She couldn't in all honesty wish they'd never met,
but the circumstances of their meeting could have
been kinder. It seemed incredible that anyone could
make such an impact on her in so short a time, and
she realized with an indrawn gasp of astonishment that
she didn't even know his name. Of all her thoughts
that was the most startling, yet why, she couldn't
imagine. Abductors aren't noted for pausing to introduce themselves before carrying off their victims. In
any case, this was no ordinary abduction case. She
suspected that Glenda would know his name.

When she had impulsively offered Glenda the loan
of her Mini and agreed to collect Glenda's car and
drive it home for her she could never in a million years
have envisaged that it would land her in a situation like
this. Days drifted by, months marched ahead, with
only the seasons changing to add any variety, then—
wham—this!

"May I know your name?"

"I'll say one thing for you, you certainly stick to your
guns."

"All right, I've had a shocking memory lapse.
Humor me."

"Maxwell Robert Bruce Ross." Although he used
an "as if you didn't know" tone, he said his name with
pride. And with complete justification. It was a good,
strong-sounding Scottish name, and how well it suited
him!

"Mr. Ross," she began tentatively, a pulse working
in her throat and making her voice quiver just a little.

"As we are going to be close companions, I think it would be better if you called me Maxwell."

"Thank you, I would prefer that." She moistened her dry lips with her tongue. "In return will you call me Gemma?"

"I would if it were your name—Glenda," he tossed back over his shoulder.

Her fingers tightened at her own helplessness. There was nothing she could do—for the moment. She didn't know how she was going to achieve this, but when she got out of this car she had to make her escape. She must not get onto the ferry, or whatever kind of boat he had arranged to be there to take them to the island he mentioned, because her chances of finding someone who would help her get away would be considerably lower there than here on the mainland. There were hundreds of islands off the coast of Scotland. The ones nearest to the mainland, the popular resorts such as Skye or Mull, might still attract a few tourists, even in winter, but if he was taking her to one of the outer islands she could consider herself truly isolated from help. The people might still cling to the ancient Gaelic and not even speak her language.

They had to leave the car at some point. Hopefully someone would be about and she could call out for assistance. All she had to do was sit tight, watch carefully for her chance, and not be afraid to seize it when it came. Constructive thought gave her a tiny thrill of elation. She was doing something, if only planning, as they sped through the night.

The moon was not up yet but the sky was full of milky-white stars. On either side the mountains loomed, their peaks permanently shrouded in snow.

"Would you go a little slower, please?" she asked, wondering how long her stomach was going to keep up with the pace.

"I know I'm pushing it a bit, but I want to catch the
tide. Anyway, I should have thought you were used to
speed."

By his tone this was obviously a reference to
Glenda's lifestyle. "Glenda might be. I'm not," she
replied steadfastly.

All that she received in reply was a terse grunt.

So they were sailing tonight, she thought hollowly,
even though her mind had already accepted this as a
strong possibility by the way he kept his foot on the
accelerator. If only a thick blanket mist, the kind that
Scotland was noted for, would come down and
obliterate the earth, so that they would have to put up
somewhere for the night. An inn or hotel, where they
would be with people who might help her.

She looked out the car window and saw no stars,
and for a moment she thought that her wish had been
granted and a sudden mist had come down. But then
she realized that the sky was blacked out because they
were traveling directly beneath a sharp overhang of
rock. The road wound round a sleeping loch before
plunging into a glen full of night shadows and an
atmosphere of doom that tingled Gemma's skin and
lifted the hairs at the nape of her neck. In daylight, no
doubt, it was a place of serene beauty, but in this milky
starlight it was full of ghosts and long-ago happenings.
The sighing of the wind was like the shuffling of
marching feet, and the shadows and grotesque shapes
formed by rock and scrub were the souls of long-dead
warriors who had trailed blood across the glen with
their acts of villainy and were chained here, unable to
find peace, forever searching to make expiation for
their sins on earth.

Gemma wasn't sorry when they left this unreal,
almost theatrical setting behind and came upon the
outskirts of a town. Houses and shops replaced the

mountain-guarded lochs and the wild, weird glens.
The shops were in darkness, their windows shuttered
for the night. The streets were empty. It was a port,
but she didn't think the ferries would be running at this
time of night, so it seemed reasonable to assume that
her captor had made special arrangements for a boat
to take them over.

He slowed down and pulled in beside the quay. He
got out of the car, locking his door, and came round to
help her out. Oh, please let someone come into view.
It was no good making a run for it unless there was
someone to run to.

After the warmth of the car the raw air took her
breath away and froze on her nose and cheeks,
making her face feel numb within seconds. She was
glad of her sheepskin coat and warm boots.

His hand clamped round her wrist, drawing her to
his side. If theirs had been a normal relationship it
would have been a protective gesture. As it was she
knew that he was holding on to her so that she
couldn't escape.

"Are you leaving the car here?" she asked as he
started to lead her away.

"I've arranged for someone to drive it home for
me."

"Your home? Do you live on the mainland, then?"

That was something else she presumably ought to
know, but he merely said, "Yes."

He wasn't forthcoming about where his home was
and it didn't seem particularly important. Besides
which, her ears had picked up the sound of footsteps.
A woman's light steps and the heavier tread of a man.
Her eyes reached forward into the night and her
breath held to see a couple braving the cold and taking
a walk. It would have delighted her more to see two
burly men, but anyone was better than no one.

She tentatively twisted her wrist; Maxwell's hold tightened and she knew that had been a mistake. The giveaway gesture had put him on his guard.

She had meant to wait until the couple came nearer before shouting out to them, but she knew that she must act at once before he did something to stop her. It was already too late. Even as she attempted to scream out for help his mouth came down on hers, blotting out the sound, including the tiny gasp of dismay she gave on realizing what a very effective way this was to prevent her from calling out for assistance.

She was inwardly blazing with fury at herself for letting him outwit her and for losing the opportunity to get help, and her eyes closed on tears of helplessness and frustration. She tried to close her mouth into a thin unyielding line, to no avail, because he was holding onto his advantage and the tenacious, silencing kiss forced her lips apart. She tried to stay immune to the invasion that was being forced upon her, reminding herself in aching desperation that he wasn't kissing her in ardor, but to shut her up. She trembled against the hard strength of him, gathering her resources and pulling herself together, then renewed her fight to break free. It was hopeless. The harder she struggled, the tighter his arms bound her, until she thought her bones would crumble. As he crushed her into submission she felt that she was being stripped of dignity, a subservient slave to the increasing pressure of his lips in that never ending kiss.

The footsteps drew level. She heard the man say, "That's one way to keep warm." The girl's reply was muffled in a giggle. Then both voices and footsteps receded into the distance. Still Maxwell's mouth was welded on hers. There was no gradual awareness to act as warning, just an explosion of sensuality ripping her apart, a burning-all-over feeling that strained her emotions to unimaginable heights of sweetness. She lost her bid to remain aloof. Her lips began to stir under his, responding of their own volition. An ecstasy she had never known before drained her will to resist.

It ended as abruptly as it began. The cold night air cut her cheek as he straightened up and she was deprived of the sheltering warmth of his face.

"Mm'm, not bad. Quite good, in fact," he taunted.

She wasn't aware that as they'd kissed she had been straining up to him on her toes until she felt her heels dropping to the ground. The demonic glint in his black-olive eyes noted this fact, to her deep humiliation, so it would be true to say that she was brought down to reality with a painful jolt.

"Didn't take the ice long to melt," he said, a slow, sarcastic smile spreading across his lips.

Stung by his sneering, despairing because he wouldn't believe that she wasn't Glenda Channing, her chin lifted as she said hotly, "Why are you so horrid to me? I haven't done anything to offend you."

He said autocratically, "When you offend my kin, you offend me."

It was one of those telling remarks her mind hungrily stored to be explored later. It had about it the ghastly echo of feudal times when clan loyalty was fierce and honor had to be upheld, when vendettas were bitter and scores settled in blood. Her thoughts made her own blood run cold, and then, just as quickly, heat up in anger. Even if Maxwell Ross thought he had just cause to seek reparation he should do so through the proper channels. They weren't in the middle ages now, and he couldn't take the law into his own hands. But he had, she thought helplessly, and she was here as proof. And it was absolutely urgent to break away from him before getting on the boat. Once they left the mainland her chances of escape would be very slim indeed.

The moon had risen without her noticing it. It was a bright silver disk illuminating the night sky. Perfect weather for sailing, she guessed bitterly, despite the intense cold.

Her ears pricked up again. She could hear something—something apart from the suck and splash of the inky dark water that was such a short distance from her feet as they continued to walk along the quayside. She could hear footsteps other than theirs.

This time she was careful to avoid straining her neck and made no giveaway tug with her fingers. The lumbering outlines of two men came into view. True, neither of them matched up to Maxwell in physique, but there were two of them, so surely they would be able to overcome him. She had no intention of making the mistake she'd made in the case of the man and the girl. She wasn't going to wait until they were nearer and be silenced by a kiss. She was going to make the break now, while she had the chance.

She could hardly believe it when she managed to wrench free of his hold, and then she was running like the wind. Her feet seemed to have found an impetus of their own, moving as swiftly as if they were mechanized.

One of the men was a pace in front of the other. She threw herself at him, tearing her breath from her lungs to gasp out, "Help me, please. I'm being kidnapped."

He laughed at her! He thought it was a joke!

"It's true. You've got to believe me."

He laughed even louder. It was a harsh, unpleasant sound, and her eyes flashed instinctively to the other man. He wasn't laughing; he looked puzzled. Would he help her?

By this time Maxwell had caught up. His hands came round her waist and she twisted her head to look up in dismay at his grinning, mocking face and she knew that the joke was on her.

The first man, younger than his companion by more than twenty years, more slightly built with slitted weasel-eyes, gave another loud guffaw and said, "It's a spirited wee lassie Mr. Ian has got for himself, Mr. Ross, sir."

They were all in league. Maxwell had let her escape because these men were his accomplices!

The older man, the one with the puzzled look on his face, said, "What's the to-do, Mr. Ross? I thought—"

"Take no notice, man. She's taken it into her head to play this tomfool game. What it amounts to is that she's changed her mind. Have you ever known a female who knows what she wants for two minutes together?"

"Now that ye mention it, sir, I haven't." Turning his eyes to Gemma he said, "It's for the best, Miss. Master Ian would wish it."

Who was Master Ian? she wondered. "It's kidnapping," she insisted furiously. "No matter what lies he tells you, it's kidnapping. If you help him, that's what you'll be aiding and abetting."

"Mr. Ross? You tell me it's not true. You said it was what she wanted. I won't be a party to kidnapping."

"She's overwrought, Angus. Anyone who can change her mind that quick can just as speedily change it back again. It will be right. In any case, man, would you rather be a party to the other?"

"No, Mr. Ross, I wouldna," Angus said, sending Gemma a sharp, admonishing look.

It didn't surprise Gemma that none of this made any sense. On the contrary, she would have been most surprised if it had.

Maxwell inquired, "How is Ian? Not that I've been away long enough for there to have been any major developments," he added, but all the same his eyes were anxious.

"No change. It's a sad thing," Angus said, his voice choked.

"It is sad," Maxwell agreed. "But he's not dead and buried yet, Angus. We must look on the bright side."

"Aye. How right ye are, sir," Angus replied readily.

The younger man seemed more interested in her than in the luckless Ian, whoever he was. His weasel-eyes looked at her in a way that was most offensive. Although it was a curious and ironic thought in the circumstances, she was glad that Maxwell was there. Had she not been under his protection she was sure that this obnoxious creature would have done more than look.

An involuntary shiver of revulsion went through her, accompanied by an unconscious drawing nearer to Maxwell Ross, a gesture that in itself brought its own crop of disturbing thoughts. She doubted if there was a woman alive who could stand this close to him and not feel a spark of something. In her case, with her lips still burning from his kiss, it was like aiming a pair of bellows at her smoldering emotions. In silencing her lips he had awakened feelings in her she hadn't known existed. She had never responded like that to Barry's kisses, and she had always sensed that some emotional stimulus was missing. From an early age she had been fed a literary diet of all the classic fairy tales and just like every other little girl she had harbored thoughts of being Sleeping Beauty awakening to the

Prince's kiss. Somehow she had twisted her fairy-tale imaginings into this nightmare reality.

Her thoughts were cut off as she found herself being bundled onto the boat. Weasel-face, who answered to the name of Andy, was mercifully not coming with them, which was something to give thanks for. His task, it seemed, was to drive Maxwell's car home for him, because he took the keys, his smirking gaze leaving her face only to stroll slowly down the length of her body. She was glad of Maxwell's arm pulling her down to sit beside him as Angus moved over to take the wheel of the boat.

As the engine throbbed into life she angled her neck to see exactly what Angus did to effect this maneuver. In the bright moonlight she would have been able to see well enough if only his back hadn't kept moving to obscure her view. She knew nothing about boats, but felt that she ought to get the measure of this one in case the opportunity arose for her to steal it, at which point she would have to find the courage to take the controls and make her way back to the mainland.

She watched the receding shoreline with angry thoughts and sinking disbelief. This couldn't be happening to her. It might have been unwitting on Glenda's part, but she had certainly got out of this very nicely. And why, she asked herself, should she have to suffer for something that Glenda had done? It was very true that she hadn't been subjected to physical violence, but there was such a thing as mental cruelty, and she was finding out that that could be worse than actual brutality. She suffered every time Maxwell looked at her as though she was something that had crawled out from under a stone. Every glance he tossed her was flecked with icy contempt. Angus's attitude to her confirmed that whatever Glenda had

done it must have been bad. He had also been giving
her some dark and disapproving looks, which, as far as
she was concerned, was pretty damning for Glenda.
She prided herself on being a reasonable judge of
character and she would have put her shirt on her
evaluation of Angus as a law-abiding, fair-minded
man, the type who wouldn't knowingly commit even
the most minor offense. Yet what he knew made it
right with his conscience to be Maxwell's accomplice.
She dismissed Andy. The only thing his involvement
confirmed was her belief that a shady character like
that would do anything for money. He was obviously
being paid, but Angus . . . he was up to his neck in it
with Maxwell because of . . . what?

And who was this Ian whose health was causing
such concern? When she had said that she was being
kidnapped and appealed to Angus for help he had
replied to the effect that it was for the best. "Master Ian
would wish it," he had said.

She remembered something else, this time a remark
of Maxwell's. "When you offend my kin, you offend
me." Was Ian his kin? Or was it a coincidence that
since the mention of Ian's name his manner toward
her had grown even colder and more condemning
than before? There was too much she didn't know,
too many gaps in the puzzle.

She turned her face to look at Maxwell and said in
entreaty, "Please, won't you tell me what this is all
about?" When he didn't answer she reaffirmed, "I am
not Glenda Channing."

"So you keep saying," he drawled, his cold tone
playing on her nerves.

"And I'll go on saying it until you believe me," she
asserted with fervor, her heart in her expression.

He grasped her by the shoulders. "Don't come that.

I am not my brother. I will not be taken in by that melting look of injured innocence."

Even through the thickness of her coat, his touch electrified her skin. "Who is your brother? Is Ian your brother?"

"As if you don't know!"

"I don't know."

It was all so hopeless. Silence fell between them and she lapsed into thought again. She had never had time for village gossip, which was often flavored for entertainment value and tended to be highly exaggerated; she had always tried to shut her ears to it and make up her own mind. The villagers didn't have a good word to say about Glenda. Unfortunately, Glenda had never gone out of her way to raise Gemma's opinion much above the one that was commonly held. She was a chip off the old block, as devious and unscrupulous in her ways as her father. There wasn't the slightest doubt in Gemma's mind that Maxwell Ross was fully justified in what he was doing, but that didn't help her.

If that wasn't enough, she realized that she had a further complication to grapple with. Not only did she find herself respecting Maxwell Ross—she admired anyone with high principles and would uphold their right to defend them to the bitter end—but she was much too conscious of him as a man. She must not let herself be drawn to him in that way. All such feelings must be stamped out at once. But how?

3

She woke with a start, expecting to see her own rose-patterned curtains at the window, framing a view of neighboring cottage chimney pots, fields where cows grazed, and softly rolling fells for the sturdy, tough-coated Dales sheep to climb. Instead her eyes met floor-length blue drapes, matching the canopy on the four-poster bed in which she lay, and the scarecrow arm of a tree, black and leafless, tapping on an unfamiliar window pane.

She sighed in despair, realizing that it hadn't been a bad dream but had really happened. Driving Glenda's car, being abducted by Maxwell Robert Bruce Ross, the most disturbing and dramatically handsome man she had ever met, meeting up with Angus and Andy, the boat ride to this remote island and eventually coming to this house—all were real.

She remembered watching Angus handle the boat, carefully memorizing the sequence of the controls in

case the boat provided her with the means of escape
—and the realization that, in his turn, Maxwell must
have been watching her in secret amusement, knowing as he did that Angus was merely dropping them off
and taking the boat back to the mainland. That had
been a severe disappointment, because she sensed
that she had found a friend in Angus. She had gauged
his age to be between forty-five and fifty, which would
have given him enough time to have learned that
things weren't always as they appeared, and she had
hoped that he would be more receptive to the truth
than Maxwell was. But no, it was not to be, and so
here she was, alone with, and the prisoner of, a man
whose strong personality matched up in every way to
his imposing name. Maxwell Robert Bruce Ross. It
had a most distinguished ring to it and positively rolled
off the tongue.

If she hadn't been at boiling point because something like this could have happened to her she might
have regarded it as an adventure. If she hadn't been
frustrated beyond endurance she would have quite
enjoyed waking up in this grand room in a bed as soft
as a powder puff and being looked down at by the
smiling faces of cherubs carved in the dark and ancient
wood. She would have taken pleasure in the warm
flannelette nightgown that by rights should have had
an accompanying mop cap and cozy woolen bed-
socks.

When he had handed the attire to her last night
mischief had prompted her to say as much to Maxwell.
He had replied darkly that he could doubtless find the
missing accessories. She had just as quickly said,
"Thank you, but no thank you," feeling that the
situation was ridiculous enough as it was.

The nightgown, Maxwell had informed her, belonged to someone called Morag. He hadn't elabo-

rated on who Morag was and she hadn't asked. She deduced that Morag was small in stature, but mighty in girth. The nightgown would have wrapped round Gemma three times and still have material to spare, but the sleeves wouldn't pull down to her wrists and the hem didn't reach her ankles. As she didn't aspire to any great height herself, a fact she had always regretted, Morag must be very short indeed.

She got out of bed, shivering in the chill air. It seemed the height of silliness to put on her boots to go to the bathroom which was along the corridor so, as she had no slippers, she went barefoot.

Washed, divested of Morag's nightgown, and wearing her own lavender wool dress, plus boots, she ventured down the stairs. Following her nose, which twitched to the loveliest smell in the world—freshly percolated coffee—she found the kitchen.

In contrast to the dark-paneled, rather awesome face of the rest of the house, the kitchen was decorated in white and a light and pleasingly delicate shade of blue, the coldness of the colors being dispelled by the homey atmosphere and the warmth given out by the stove.

It was blissful to close the door and leave the drafts behind, a thought quickly reversed on seeing Maxwell's expression, which was several degrees below zero.

"Good morning," he said icily. "I trust you slept well?"

"Very well, thank you."

"Breakfast is coming up."

"Just coffee, please, if it's all the same to you."

Obviously it wasn't. He placed a steaming bowl of porridge before her. "Eat."

"Now look here—"

"No, you look here." He towered above her, his

dark eyes glowering down into hers. "You'll eat that of your own accord or I'll force-feed you."

"What concern is it of yours whether I eat or not?" she spluttered in amazement.

"I made it my concern when I brought you here. I have taken on the responsibility of your welfare and I will see to it that you eat three good meals a day, get at least eight hours sleep each night and your daily quota of exercise."

"This situation gets sillier as it goes on. I will not submit to your ruling. Who do you think you are that you can order me about? I absolutely refuse to—"

He made a menacing move toward her and she hurriedly picked up her spoon and transferred a little of the porridge to her mouth. Even eaten while choking on rage she had to admit to herself that it was good, but she would not give him the satisfaction of knowing this and continued to pull a face with every successive mouthful.

"Bacon, eggs, and kidneys all right to follow?" he said.

"It most certainly is not. It is not the hallmark of a good host to bully his houseguests like this," she complained.

"You're hardly a houseguest."

"That evens the score, because you're hardly a good host. You are, in fact, an unprincipled barbarian. I'm not used to eating huge breakfasts, so while it's just possible that you might force me to eat one I very much doubt if even you could make me keep it down. Now, may I have some coffee, please?"

She got it. He sat down opposite her and devoured bacon, kidneys and two perfectly fried eggs, presumably meant for her, in dour silence.

She made no attempt to break it, but drank her coffee in brooding contemplation. The silence wasn't ended until he'd finished eating and she had drunk a second cup of coffee.

Rising from her chair, she said, "I'll do the washing up." But instead of getting on with the task she paused hesitantly by the table, unable to resist venting her frustration. "It would be something to understand the situation. Won't you tell me what I'm supposed to have done to earn this fate? Or, should I say, as I can't seem to convince you that I really am Gemma Coleridge, what Glenda Channing has done?"

Even before he uttered one single word the wry twisting of his mouth indicated that her plea was going to be ignored. "There's an apron of Morag's hanging on a peg at the back of the pantry door. Pity to spoil that pretty dress." He spoke slowly while casting a speculative and unhurried eye along the length of her.

He was deliberately doing this to undermine her, of course. It occurred to her that some men got a perverted pleasure in embarrassing a girl with a too-long look, but she didn't think it was that which had motivated his prolonged study. It wasn't that sort of appraisal and, stranger still, the embarrassment was all his for enjoying looking at her. His expression quickly went guarded, but not before she had seen his flicker of interest followed closely by something that seemed to resemble startled shame. Which made no more sense than anything else did. Why should he feel uncomfortable about what was, after all, a very understandable reaction? What was shameful about looking at a woman and finding her attractive?

"Is Morag a domestic or family?" she asked, a surge of pleasure whipping through her because he'd set out to disconcert her and had ended up by disconcerting himself. That must be the reason for her delight. Surely she wasn't foolish enough to be glad that he wasn't as indifferent to her as he would care to make out? That could only serve to make her position here more dangerous than it already was.

"Domestic, I suppose." A few seconds elapsed before he elaborated on his reply. "She's been with us so long that she seems more like family." He had quite recovered himself now and the return of his equilibrium was marked by the resumption of that scathing tone she found so intolerable. "We might be here for some time, and as you didn't bring a change of clothing with you—"

"Was I likely to have brought anything with me?" she cut in, retaliating in a rush of annoyance, matching his sarcasm. "I'm not in the habit of waking up and saying to myself, 'I'm likely to be kidnapped today, so I'll pack a suitcase on the off chance.'"

"As I was saying—as you didn't bring anything with you, I'll scout round and find something else for you to wear."

"Of Morag's?" she said, unable to resist that poke as an impression of Morag's short but voluminous nightgown flashed into her mind.

A similar picture must have presented itself to him, because the dourness of his mouth almost, but not quite, slid into a smile. It would have been the first proper smile she'd seen and she was disappointed when his lips tightened again.

"No. Of Fiona's."

"And Fiona is . . . ?"

"Very clever."

"Is she?" she inquired, thinking what a strange reply that was.

"She's not in the least academic. She's got more going for her in the way of looks than brains. I meant your stratagem. Very cunning of you to pretend not to know who Morag and Fiona are when Ian must have mentioned them to you on many occasions."

His face went sad and she knew that she'd lost him to Ian who was apparently, she remembered, his brother. She also recalled the inquiry he'd made about Ian's condition, which seemed to be causing some concern. And then his gritty retaliation to Angus's doleful expression of sympathy, "He's not dead and buried yet." Was Ian expected to die? Something obviously had happened to him. He'd either been struck by illness or accident. And Glenda, apparently, was supposed to know Ian. Did Maxwell blame Glenda for Ian's misfortune? There had to be a connection somewhere, but what was it?

At that point Maxwell announced brusquely that he was going outside to chop some logs. She washed the dishes and put them away, hung the tea-towel to dry, and lifted her eyes from the kitchen sink to look out the window at a suggestion of descending mist, the sort she'd prayed would come down yesterday with sufficient vengeance to make sailing impossible.

The vaporous swirls parted for a moment, an unseen hand dragging back a curtain, to give her a brief view of brooding purple mountains with their frozen caps of snow that never melted. Bleak, yes, yet in some indefinable way a compellingly beautiful scene, its stark majesty softened by the gentle drift of daytime mist.

Not caring that Maxwell might have made the necessity to chop logs an excuse to get away from her, she pulled on her sheepskin coat and opened the door. It was a prison without locks for the simple reason that there was nowhere to escape to.

Standing beside a tidy pile of logs—excuse or not he'd got on with the task—Maxwell looked up in inquiry as she slammed the door shut behind her.

"I thought I'd like to stretch my legs and see something of your island. Has it a name?"

"It's called Iola," he said, nodding at what he apparently accepted as a sound idea. He threw down the ax. They fell into step together, Maxwell leading the way.

Talk was sparse. The lack of it didn't seem to bother Maxwell in the least. The expression "taciturn Scot" suited him admirably, along with a few more adjectives she could think of without any great difficulty. She had fun bringing them to mind. Feudal. Stubborn. Impossible. Bossy. And bigoted beyond belief. The poor girl who married him would have her work cut out. Which raised another question. Was he married already? Or engaged? Perhaps to the mysterious Fiona?

In the preliminary stages of getting to know a person the conversation generally takes the form of question and answer. Stubbornly holding the conviction that she was Glenda Channing, he was convinced she knew all the answers already through her relationship with his brother, Ian. Because of this, any question she put forward was received in anger. She could have resorted to social chitchat, she supposed, making some banal comment about the weather, but she was no more the type to talk for talking's sake than he was, so she remained silent. If he wanted conversation it would be safer to let him initiate it.

Strangely enough, it wasn't a strained, separate silence, but a shared one, enfolding them in a deep pocket of content as they tramped along together. On her side she was engrossed in the sleeping beauty of the island with its trees and mountains and gray, glittering lochs. She sensed two things. First, that the full force of winter was hovering on the horizon, ready to come in fast, wiping out this bland calm, threatening ice and snow. And, secondly, that Maxwell was soaking up memories of years past.

She was totally unsurprised, yet at the same time pleased, to be allowed into his memory, to hear him say, "It looks different."

"Different?"

"In winter."

"Don't you come in winter?"

"Used to. Not recently. It's come to be regarded as a spring-to-autumn retreat. But in my grandparents' time . . ."

"Yes?"

"It was usual to come all the year round. Iola was populated then, and no one needed much excuse for a *ceilidh*. That's a gathering where yarns are spun and vast quantities of food and drink are consumed and everyone is expected to contribute his or her party piece."

"Even a Sassenach like me knows what a *ceilidh* is. I bet you had fun."

"We did. From Burns Supper to the most minor family event, you name it and we celebrated it. The men in Highland dress, the women in pretty gowns with tartan sashes, and Hamish McBride on the pipes because he had the best ear and could handle the 'warbles'—the grace notes. He was a character, all right. Couldn't read a single note of music, but he could throw the drones over his shoulder and pull out a tune to set the feet tapping." The vibrancy in Maxwell's voice brought it vividly to life for her. She felt the warmth and the camaraderie and was in step with the music and the merry-making. And then he was off on another tack. "When the small loch froze, out would come our skates. We'd test the ice daily, hourly, sometimes, in our impatience for it to hold our weight. Once, Ian—" He stopped abruptly. The magic spell was broken as he said his brother's name and recalled who she was, or, more correctly, who he thought she was, and his grim expression was like a door slamming in her face. And it was all the more painful after being let in, even briefly.

She found herself damning Glenda Channing for whatever she'd done to Maxwell's brother, and so spoiling the harmony of the moment for her. Why, oh why did she have to get involved in Glenda's invidious affairs? And yet, if she hadn't got involved, she wouldn't have had reason to meet Maxwell and that wouldn't have suited either.

His stride quickened and she had to put in twice as many steps to keep up with him as they climbed out of the glen, following a line of Scots pine with trunks like the foremasts of sailing ships, deep-rooted to stand up to the fiercest gale. In contrast, the alders, birch, and rowan were pliant and at the will of the wind, bending before and not standing up to the gales.

The mist turned spiteful. Its gentle softening-the-landscape effect became a damp obliterating blanket and Maxwell said it would be as well to turn back. Several times she stumbled and almost lost her footing on the rough and unfamiliar ground. He reduced his pace, but not once did he offer a steadying hand. But whether it was from repugnance, because he couldn't stomach the thought of touching her, or because he was afraid to touch her because he was not total master of his feelings, she had no way of knowing.

By the time they arrived back at the house Gemma felt very cold and sorry for herself indeed. Warm as her sheepskin coat was, it only reached just below her hips, leaving the lower part of her dress exposed to the damp.

Looking her over, Maxwell said in grudging apology, "I should have found you something more suitable to wear sooner, rather than later. I'll sort something out now. But first I'll put some soup on. Only the packet variety, I'm afraid, but it will serve the purpose of warming you through.''

Despite his disparaging opinion of packet soup it smelled delicious as it simmered gently on the stove. Perhaps it was something to do with the air, but she was looking forward to sampling it. She also felt that she could do full justice to one of the large steaks which Maxwell had taken out of the deep freeze that morning.

While he went to find her some alternative attire she took a curious peep into the freezer and gasped to see it so well stocked. He had mentioned that nowadays the house was only visited between spring and autumn, so the freezer wouldn't be in all-year-round use. When the house was unoccupied she imagined that the electricity would be switched off, in which case the freezer had been stocked in anticipation of their arrival. If the amount of food was anything to go by, he intended to keep her here for quite some time.

He came back with an assortment of garments. Jeans and sweaters, a pleated skirt, and a cozy red housecoat, the latter being just the thing to keep drafts at bay. She could tell at a glance that the owner of these clothes was considerably taller than she was. She held the housecoat in front of her and it swept the floor.

Glenda, she recalled, was exactly her height. What was she thinking? She pondered for a moment. Everything about Glenda's kidnap had been meticulously planned. He hadn't grabbed her on impulse; every move had been well thought out in advance. He had known the road that Glenda would take to get home, even, Gemma suspected, the approximate time she would be there. Angus and Andy had been waiting at the quayside with a boat to bring them to the island, which had been visited beforehand and got ready for them. He had gone out of his way to see that her stay here would be as comfortable as he could possibly make it. Whatever else she had to say about him she could not fault him on that count. He had given her that lovely room, with that gorgeous four-poster bed, and he obviously meant to feed her well. His every action served to prove that her comfort and well-being were of paramount importance. It made her wonder why he hadn't thought to stock up with clothes in Glenda's size. It seemed a curious omission in view of everything else.

Or hadn't it been an omission? Could it be that that stupid comment of his about her not bringing a change of clothing with her hadn't been such a stupid comment at that?

What was she getting at? His assumption that Glenda would come prepared with her suitcase packed would suggest that Glenda was in on the plot.

"Any good?" he inquired, looking dubiously from the garments to Gemma as if he'd only just realized that their rightful owner was so much taller than she was.

"Better than nothing." She hoped she didn't sound ungracious. It was apparent that he'd done the best he could. "These are Fiona's, I believe you said. Will she mind?"

"Fiona? Not her. She's a generous soul; she won't mind in the least. I'm sure she'd be only too happy to help out."

His reply was touched with proprietorial pride, which made her wonder again about his relationship with Fiona.

"I could do with a belt, to take in the waist and hitch up the skirt." She frowned in pretend preoccupation with the length of the housecoat, attempting to cover up the unreasonable pang she had experienced at the way he said Fiona's name.

"I'll dig something out."

"No hurry," she said indifferently.

She asked him if he wanted help in getting their lunch ready. When he declined she didn't press the matter but went upstairs for a trying-on session.

Everything was much too big, just as she had known it would be. The waistband of the skirt didn't fit snugly; the same applied to the jeans, which sagged and bagged and had hopelessly long legs. She wondered if Fiona would mind if she made free with a needle and cotton and put in a few discreet tucks.

She changed back into her dress and trotted down to the kitchen to put this question to Maxwell. He said Fiona wouldn't mind, and produced a work basket.

It was old and had obviously seen many years of faithful use. There was a handle on the lid which she lifted to reveal a pin-neat, velvet-lined interior in a pretty shade of deep rose. From the tidy rows of every color thread imaginable she made her choice.

She didn't have to ask; she knew instinctively that the work basket had belonged to Maxwell's grandmother. She sat in the big pine rocker, which had the feel of having been Maxwell's grandmother's favorite chair, her head bent industriously over her sewing. The homeliness of her actions took her back to their recent walk—more particularly to how Maxwell had mellowed as he let her into his life as it used to be, with all the comings and goings he knew as a boy. The warmth of his memories wrapped round her and she felt a nostalgic longing for the days of her own childhood and the carefree years before she lost her parents. She had been a tiny afterthought, a huge disruption of her parents' lives, coming as she did in her mother's late thirties, when all thoughts of having the child they had so desperately desired and prayed for had long since ceased. She had enjoyed her parents for close on twenty years. Her father had been older than her mother and when he died her mother had been inconsolable, and a few months later she had also passed on. A tear pricked her eye and she bent her head lower until she felt more composed.

If she hadn't been so engulfed in her thoughts she might have sensed that Maxwell was looking at her, the harshness of his features softened by the puzzled expression that had come to his face.

She wished he didn't think so badly of her. She knew that she wasn't perfect by any means. She had a quick temper and an unexpected jealous streak that needed watching, which she hadn't known about until he started talking about Fiona. She made mistakes—didn't everyone?—and had abided by the consequences. That was perfectly fair. She didn't mind paying for her own mistakes and even held the belief that it made her a stronger person. But she objected most forcefully to shouldering the burden of someone else's mistakes, misdeeds, or whatever heading most appropriately fitted Glenda's mysterious transgression.

Her head came up. "Maxwell?"

"Yes?"

"I'm right, aren't I, in thinking that we're not connected to the mainland by phone and that we're cut off from the outside world?"

"You're right about the phone, but we're not completely cut off. We do have contact—by boat, remember? Angus will bring a regular supply of fresh produce plus, of course, things like newspapers."

"Mm—that's what I was getting at—newspapers. Do you agree that Clifford Channing wouldn't take his daughter's disappearance lying down? If she was missing it would be reported in the newspapers, right?"

His eyes narrowed and he adopted a tone of chilling tolerance as he said, "I'll go along with that."

He was talking down to her, pandering to her as he would a child. He was doing this quite deliberately to humiliate her, and she wondered if anyone had ever been able to disrupt his impregnable calm. She could have taken it better if he'd blown his top with her rather than spoken condescendingly to her.

"And when it isn't . . . ?" She refused to be incited to anger, although it took all the composure she could muster to match his control. "When there's not one word about her disappearance in the newspapers, then will you believe that I'm not Glenda Channing?"

One black eyebrow lifted derisively. "I would certainly have grounds for a serious re-think, but that possibility is hardly likely to arise. You are Glenda Channing and your name will be blazoned across the front page of every newspaper to prove it. The press will have a ball."

How could he be so positive? So calm in his disbelief? If only she could shake him out of his righteous complacency, rouse him to anger—anything but this glacial smoothness that set her teeth on edge.

"You won't even admit that you just conceivably might be wrong." Despite her good intentions she was biting back frustration and temper.

"Isn't this conversation rather a waste of time?" he drawled, evincing lazy boredom.

"Obviously. Because you're like those mountains out there; you never melt. You can't see the truth when it's staring you in the face. But that's not important anymore. It doesn't matter who you think I am. I demand that you come out of the Dark Ages, stop this petty vengeance, and take me home. Hasn't it occurred to you that someone might be worrying about me?"

The sardonic twist of his mouth summed up his grim satisfaction in being able to agree with her. "I should imagine that your parents will be extremely worried. Your father, in particular, will be tearing his hair out by the roots because his carefully laid plans have gone awry. Please forgive me, but as his influence over you is partly to blame for my having to bring you here, I can't feel too much regret about that."

"I forgive you nothing!" she spat at him. "You can't feel regret because you're incapable of human emotion. You're inhuman and bigoted. I've never met anyone like you and I hate you for what you're doing to me. I know I've got a temper, but for the most part I manage to keep it under control. But you goad me with that look of yours. I must have reacted the first time you looked at me like that and so you know just what to do to get at me. Just be careful you don't give me such a weapon, because if you do I'll turn it on you. I'll . . ." The threat died on her lips, swallowed in a gasp of dismay, because she could not envisage a time when she would have the upper hand. No one, man, woman, child or beast, would ever get the better of him.

She achieved something. The "look" left his eyes to be replaced by concern.

"You're getting distraught. It can't be good for you."

"*Getting?*" she questioned with rising hysteria. "I *am* distraught. The only tiny bit of comfort I can find in the whole of this stupid situation is that my parents won't be worried. They died over two years ago, so at least they're spared that heartache. But there are people who care about me and who will worry and it isn't fair to put them to this kind of distress. There's Miss Davies at the library, where I work. My neighbors. Even Barry, in his own way."

"Barry?" he queried, his tone sharpening.

She didn't know why she had tossed out Barry's name. If he was tormented at all it would be because he didn't care for puzzles and he would be mystified by her disappearance, but she was sure he didn't care deeply enough about her to endure any real suffering. The relationship between them had been based on friendship. No vital spark or lovers' clashes, no heights and depths of feelings, no flights from tenderness to passion. The realization that there could be no shared future for them had been coming on gradually, yet for all that the moment of impact took her by surprise and stole her concentration. Therefore she wasn't giving much attention to what was going on behind the stony facade of Maxwell's face and she answered his question as to who Barry was in vague indifference. "A friend."

"A man friend?"

"Obviously."

His face underwent an alarming change. The black rage in his dark olive eyes made her jerk back in sheer astonishment. Not in a million years would she have thought that the mention of Barry's name would foment such feeling. How ludicrous! After all her attempts to get under his skin and rouse him to this state of anger she had fallen upon the means by accident. Barry, dull, staid, slightly pompous Barry! It was so amazing that she almost laughed out loud.

"You haven't been playing fast and loose with Ian, have you?"

He sounded too savage for her to crow openly about her triumph, but she couldn't prevent a little

flicker of satisfaction from coming to her gray eyes as
she said emphatically, "I don't know Ian, so how
could I play fast and loose with him?"

"Have you slept with Barry?"

"Now really!" As her eyes slid away from his, as
though concealing something, she realized that she
was enjoying taunting him. But she would have
enjoyed it a whole lot more if she hadn't begun to
question the wisdom of provoking him to greater fury.
Yet why should she back down? And why was he
attaching such importance to the possibility that she
might have gone to bed with Barry? "You surely don't
expect me to tell you that. It's much too personal."

"I do, and you will. Have you slept with him?
Answer me!"

"No. I don't see why I should."

"Then I'll have to provide you with a reason,
won't I?"

He grabbed her by the arms and pulled her out of
the chair so fiercely that it crashed back on its rockers,
collided with the table, catching the edge of the work
basket, and began to rock wildly backward and forward. Cotton reels, needles, pins, scissors, a colorful
assortment of buttons, all the ingredients of a well-
stocked work basket flew everywhere.

"I will not succumb to brutality," she said, quivering
with indignation, the sense of injustice she was feeling
reaching an all-time high so that it not only came to
her aid but overcame her fear of his anger. "Let me
go!" she demanded.

But her defiance earned her a severe shaking and
his fingers bit deeper into her arms; she thought that if
he held her any tighter her bones would crack. In the
end she had to cry out in anguish. "Stop . . . you're
hurting me!"

"God in Heaven!" His ejaculation was ground out in frustration and it was harsh and unrepentant. "I'll hurt you a whole lot more if you don't speak up."

He was no longer the obdurate mountain with its frozen cap. Not only had she melted the ice off the top, but she had caused a volcano to erupt.

"Damn you, Maxwell Ross!" she sobbed, closing her eyes on a wave of weakness born of despair. "I haven't slept with Barry. There, you've got it out of me. I hope you're satisfied!"

"I would be if I was convinced that you were telling the truth, that you're not lying about this just as you've lied about everything else. You'd better be telling the truth." His tone was vitriolic. "That's one complication I can do without."

4

Angus came the following day with fresh produce and several newspapers.

"Dump everything on the table," Maxwell instructed, his eyes urgently searching the older man's face in a questioning way that did not require words.

Sorrowfully, Angus shook his head. "The same. The laddie is still very poorly. Perhaps tomorrow when I come I'll have brighter news."

"I hope so, Angus. I hope so. Cup of tea and a bite to eat?"

"Aye. That would be most acceptable."

"I'll see to it," Gemma said and was rewarded by the kindly smile that Angus sent her way.

She cut hefty man-sized slices of bread for sandwiches and raided the various cake tins in the pantry which someone had thoughtfully filled in anticipation of their arrival. She wondered whether to set a cup for herself and, after a moment's thought, decided it would be in order. The talk wasn't of a personal nature; it seemed to be concerned with the business of Maxwell's estate. She gathered that Angus worked for Maxwell and held a position of some importance. It didn't take long to realize that there were strong links of friendship between the two men based on a long acquaintance.

While Angus was there Maxwell kept a bright face. But when he'd gone he slumped into the big leather wing chair that was drawn up to the log fire in the main room, his face in his hands. She found it difficult to hold hatred in her heart for this man despite the fact that he was keeping her here against her will and that his manner, for the most part, was so cold toward her that it drove her to the brink of desperation. She realized just how great an emotional strain he was under. He cared deeply for his brother, that much was obvious. Although there was still such a lot she didn't understand, and the reason for her kidnapping was a complete mystery to her, she felt that he had been following the dictates of his heart. It might seem wrong to the outside world, but he had done what he thought was right, and who could condemn a man for being true to himself? Not she. As she looked at the hurt angle of that bent black head a stirring of compassion went through her, a tiny ache that he was not as invulnerable as he cared to make out. Although nothing could alleviate the frustration of being held prisoner, there was no animosity in her entire being toward him, and she wished she could do something to help him, if only to put her hands on the strong column of his neck and massage away the coiled knots of tension. So great was this longing to touch him that she actually took a step toward him before retracting in horror on realizing what she had almost done. She didn't like his brooding silence and wondered if she should speak to him, but for the time being decided against that as well. Yet she was strangely disinclined to leave him alone in his misery, and so she slid unobtrusively into the companion chair on the other side of the hearth, making her presence known by gently rustling the pages of one of the newspapers which Angus had brought.

It was the signal for his head to jerk up. The lost, bewildered look because something like this could be happening to him and his disappeared as he regarded her harshly. His countenance, reminding her as it did of his predecessors' meting out revenge in bygone days when clan loyalty was fierce, made her straighten involuntarily and square her shoulders against the onslaught she knew was coming.

"Don't exult," he flung at her in bitterness.

Her hackles rose. What kind of person did he think she was? Did he hold her in such low esteem that he thought she would find pleasure in his pain?

"It's too soon to have got into the newspapers yet," he snarled.

Then she realized that she had judged him too quickly. He wasn't referring to his distress over his brother. He was telling her not to crow because there was no mention yet of Glenda's disappearance. She wouldn't know either way because she'd only made a token gesture of turning over the pages to let him know she was there. She had been too engrossed in her own thoughts to take in a single word.

"Even if Glenda had disappeared, it seems probable to imagine that *Mr. Channing* would wait a day or so for some word about her before making it public knowledge," she said with deliberate emphasis.

His mouth turned sardonic. "That's right. *Your father* will stew for a few days, waiting for the kidnapper to get in touch with him, because the first thought that will spring to mind is that you're being held for ransom." He showed no charity or mercy for a father's bitter anguish. Stony indifference would have been preferable to the gloating twist of his mouth as he said, "He won't dare to antagonize anyone or do anything to jeopardize his chances of getting you back. Every time the letter box clicks or the phone rings he'll break out in a cold sweat."

He was reveling in the thought. How could he be so without human feelings? And to think that a few moments ago she had actually felt sorry for him.

"It won't enter his mind that you came of your own free will. He'll think it inconceivable that you decided to stand up to him and go into voluntary hiding."

"I did not come voluntarily."

Clifford Channing might not rate in anyone's books as Mr. Good Guy. For all she knew he might have done all the unspeakable things gossip accused him of doing. But there was one thing she did know for certain: his love for his daughter was beyond question. His life revolved round her. Nothing he could have done, short of murder, was bad enough to merit this kind of punishment.

She realized she was getting het-up for nothing, reacting as if it had really happened. Glenda had not been kidnapped and so Clifford Channing was not going through that kind of mental torture. Right at this moment Glenda was very probably sitting across from her father, enjoying a conversation with him, blissfully ignorant of the fact that but for a lucky mischance (lucky for Glenda, if not for her) she wouldn't be there.

Angus came again the next day with another pile of newspapers and provisions. They both knew that none of the newspapers would contain a report of

Glenda's disappearance, Maxwell because he considered it still too early for Clifford Channing to act and expected him to play a waiting game, Gemma because she knew Glenda wasn't missing.

But before glancing at a newspaper they had both anxiously searched Angus's face for a spark of a smile that would suggest an improvement in Ian's condition. The compassion Gemma felt was none the less real for not knowing Ian. She would have grieved for any young life hanging in the balance.

Angus said somberly, "The same, Mr. Ross, before you ask. I'm sorry I canna bring better."

"I know you are, Angus. Take the provisions through to the kitchen, will you? If you talk nicely to Miss Channing I'm sure she'll put the kettle on for a brew up."

"Of course," Gemma said, rising to her feet, for once not arguing with Maxwell that Channing was not her name.

She could have managed to carry the things through to the kitchen without troubling Angus, and it was on the tip of her tongue to say this, but then she realized that Maxwell had made this excuse to get a few moments on his own.

It further occurred to her that there might be some advantage in having Angus to herself for a short time. He viewed her with a certain wariness, but because he was not as closely involved he didn't have the same bitter antagonism toward her that Maxwell had. There was such a lot she wanted to know. If she worded her questions carefully Angus might give her the answers that Maxwell was withholding on the grounds that she was supposed to know them already.

It was a puzzle to know why Maxwell was keeping her here, what Ian's condition was and how he came to be in it, and how close Glenda was—or had been—to Ian. Pretty close, judging by Maxwell's anger when she had mentioned Barry's name. He had gone berserk at the thought that she—that is, Glenda —had been two-timing Ian. His insistence on knowing whether or not she'd slept with Barry had been frightening. It might have been understandable if it had been Ian who flew into a rage at the possibility of her being on intimate terms with another man, but for a mere brother to get uptight about it made no sense at all. What had he said about it? "That's one complication I can do without." What on earth had he meant?

While waiting for the kettle to boil Gemma unpacked the dairy products, transferring the brown, new-laid eggs to the egg rack, and then she exclaimed in delight over the crusty loaves, a rich Dundee cake, and a batch of scones.

Angus beamed, bright pride in his eyes at Gemma's words of praise. "My Morag thought the cake tins might need replenishing. She's a grand wee cook."

So it was Morag's baking they had been sampling.

"Your Morag?" she queried.

"Aye. It's a handy arrangement to have husband and wife working for ye. Morag housekeeps for the laird and I'm his factor on the estate."

"The laird?"

"The laird of Glenross." As Gemma's eyebrows retained their puzzled lift he added, his weathered face showing surprise at the necessity, "Mr. Maxwell Ross, his father being dead these ten years past."

She was not surprised to find out that Maxwell was the laird of Glenross. He carried the authority of his title in his autocratic manner. "And Mr. Ross's mother?"

"She predeceased the old Laird by some five years. I suppose that you and Mr. Ian had other things to talk about," he said, as though answering his own perplexity, "but I'd a' thought with the wedding date set and everything, ye'd ken about that."

"You'd be surprised how little I do know, Angus."

So Glenda was engaged to be married to Ian Ross, and the wedding already arranged.

"Perhaps that's to be expected," Angus said, springing to the defense of those who hadn't told her the things he thought she ought to know. "The haste of it all fair took my breath away. You'll pardon me for not moving with the times, like."

His loyalty was commendable. She made a mental note not to speak out against any member of the Ross clan, knowing it would earn this same touchy response. Running parallel was the thought that Angus was censuring her for something and that she had just been politely told off.

Her mind buzzing with speculation, she said, "The wedding will have to be postponed now that Ian is in hospital."

Angus replied tersely, the disapproval even more deeply ingrained in his voice, as if he suspected her of flippancy, "The poor laddie can no get to the kirk in the wretched state he's in. Him on his back and his mind addled with all the drugs that are being pumped into him. Not knowing, and them not daring to tell him for fear he canna take the shock, that he'll spend the rest of his life on his back, never to walk again. I'm glad to hear that Mr. Ross has talked ye round."

"In what way?"

"What you said just now about postponing the wedding. In the letter, the one you sent to the hospital, you wrote that the wedding was off because you

couldn't face spending the rest of your life with a—"
the voice broke, the eyes condemned—"with a cripple."

She gasped. *"Oh!"* Her hand went to her mouth in
horror at the cruelty of anyone writing such a letter to
a desperately ill man. There wasn't anything Angus
could have said that would have shocked her more
and she found herself nodding in violent feeling and
total agreement with what he had to say next.

"Mr. Ross didn't think he could take that on top of
everything else. The laddie was pulled out of that
mangled car more dead than alive. It's a miracle that
he's rallied this long. The master kept a bedside vigil
for days, although there was little he could do there
except get in the way of the nursing staff. I was with
him when he read your letter. It was addressed to Mr.
Ian, of course, but Mr. Ross quite rightly took it upon
himself to open it. Maybe you didn't know that?"

"No, Angus, I didn't know that."

Just as she didn't know how anyone, even someone
as hard and self-centered as Glenda Channing, could
add to a man's distress by casting him off when he
most needed her. Her mind exploded with criticism
and reproach that Glenda could write such a brutal
letter to a man facing the prospect of being crippled
forever, a man fighting for his life! She shuddered at
the consequences it could have had if Maxwell hadn't
intercepted the letter and Ian had pulled round suffi-
ciently to read it. Such a bitter blow could have
finished him off, deprived him of the one thing that is
sometimes even more vital for survival than surgery or
medication, the will to live. She was beginning to
understand now why Maxwell had brought her here.

Angus seemed to confirm her thoughts as he said,
"Even if you couldn't bring yourself to marry the
laddie, Mr. Ross was determined to make you stand

by him until he was over the worst and then, he said, if you were still of the same mind, you could let him down lightly when he was more able to take it."

And rightly, too. If she'd got a spark of compassion or decency in her, Glenda wouldn't have walked out on Ian, the man she was supposed to love. She must have professed to love him to have promised to marry him. But wasn't all this rather strange, something not quite as it should be? Why the furtive haste to arrange the wedding that Angus had hinted at? Why the secrecy surrounding the engagement? Gemma would have thought that it would have been officially announced and marked by an engagement party. The Channings were noted for the flamboyancy of their parties, which they threw at the drop of a hat. Glenda's engagement would certainly have rated a party. It was well known in the village that Glenda had some man in tow, but then, she always did. If the name of the current one was known Gemma hadn't heard it. And not one hint of an impending engagement had been breathed; she would swear to it, because she certainly couldn't have missed that. And yet, according to Angus, the wedding date had been set. Something definitely did not add up.

She sought Angus's gaze, but it slid away from her and her eyes fixed on the two cross lines between his brows. The certain knowledge came to her that it didn't add up because she didn't know it all. There was something, a key factor, that would link everything together and supply the correct answer. She had got plenty of information out of Angus and she felt that she could have got more if only she'd known how to go about it. She didn't know the words to use, the line to take to trick him into telling her the last vital bit.

Giving up the struggle, she made the tea and set the tray, adding Morag's splendid Dundee cake.

To appease her own curiosity, since this question had nothing at all to do with the concerns of Glenda Channing, she asked reflectively, "Angus, who is Fiona?"

"Miss Fiona? A distant relative, a kind of niece the old Laird and his lady were fond of. I suppose you might say that she took the place of the daughter they never had and so she practically grew up at Glenross."

"Is that so," Gemma replied thoughtfully with a speedy and quite distinct lightening of her heart.

She carried the tray through into the main room where Maxwell was, with Angus walking on ahead to open doors for her.

"Ah, that looks good," Maxwell said, rousing himself from his inertia. The tautness was still on his features, betraying his inner pain, which in turn burned her heart like a stabbing flame. In her imagination she took his face in her hands and smoothed the strain and anguish away with her caring fingers, giving him back his tranquillity and calm. She ached for him, for what he was suffering now, and she admired him for the measures he had taken to protect his brother from further disillusionment, even though it was causing her considerable distress.

At the moment Ian was apparently heavily sedated, but when he came fully round, if he ever did, Glenda should be there to give him the impetus to pull through. But if she couldn't make Maxwell believe that she wasn't Glenda, when Ian opened his eyes from his drugged semi-comatose condition it wouldn't be upon Glenda's lovely face they rested; he would find himself looking at a complete stranger. It was obvious to her that Maxwell intended to keep her a prisoner until he could take her to Ian's bedside, which would be whenever Ian was well enough to receive her. The truth would then come out and Maxwell would never forgive himself for making such an appalling mistake.

She had to get away, for both Ian's and Maxwell's sakes as well as her own. She had to talk to Glenda and make her see reason. If the case was put to her fairly, without undue emotional pressure, surely even Glenda wouldn't be so hard-hearted as to deny Ian a few more weeks, or months, of thinking they were still engaged and going to be married. It wouldn't hurt her to wait until he was strong enough to be told the truth. And then, when he could take it, she could break it very gently to him that she couldn't go through with the wedding. The fact that her love hadn't proved strong enough meant that Ian was better off without her, and because he was Maxwell's brother he must have some of his strength of character; he would accept this when he was well enough and his mind was reasoning properly.

But how was she to get away? Then she remembered her first idea of taking the boat if the opportunity arose. Dare she, knowing nothing at all about boats, even if she could manage to sneak out and make her way down to the landing stage where Angus would have moored it without being observed? Did she really have a choice?

She contained herself until the tea had been drunk and a portion of the cake eaten, then loaded the crockery back onto the tray and took it through to the kitchen. That had got her out of the room, but to get her sheepskin coat out of the cloaks' cupboard in the hall meant having to pass the door again. Maxwell was like a cat, alert to her every movement, and fetching it would be a risk. But she decided it would be a greater risk to her health to contemplate taking the boat out without its protective warmth.

The hall floor, made up of hand-hewn planks, was partially covered with rugs. She could use them as stepping stones to muffle the sound of her footsteps. Just the same, she took the precaution of removing her boots and carrying them. The cloaks' cupboard was situated to the right of the main door. The pale, wintry sunshine filtered through the two small-paned windows set on either side of the door, glancing off the beamed ceiling and the somber brown walls hung with tapestries and hunting trophies. A moose's head looked down at her in stern disapproval, marking her cautious progress. She hoped that Maxwell and Angus were too deep in conversation to observe the creak the ancient hinges made as she inched open the cloaks' cupboard door and grabbed her coat. She contemplated leaving the door open to save a repeat of the noise, but decided against it. The open door would be the first thing Maxwell saw on coming out of the main room and his suspicions would be immediately alerted. Without that tell-tale sign he would think she was either upstairs or still in the kitchen, and she needed all the advantages she could get to work out how to start the boat. The protesting hinges again made the grating sound. She waited a moment and her heart thumped against her rib cage. Her held breath burned tightly in her throat before she expelled it in a sigh of relief as she let herself out the main door, where she pulled her boots back on, tucking the turned-up legs of Fiona's jeans into them, and set off at a cracking pace.

She arrived at the boat, her cheeks red from the intense cold and the exertion of running. Before untying it from its moorings she thought it best to step aboard and see if she could figure out the controls. It was more than a step, actually, it was a heart-in-the-mouth jump. The first hurdle over, she gave herself a moment to regain her balance and get used to the motion of the boat before going over to the wheel.

She was biting her lip in absorbed confusion over the instrument panel, wondering which lever to pull and which knob to turn, and she didn't hear the step behind her announcing an alien presence. The first intimation she had that she wasn't alone came when a hand touched her arm. She jerked away in revulsion, just as if her senses had darted ahead of her reasoning and told her that it was someone to cringe from. She swung round and looked in dismay into Andy's weasel-eyes.

"Going somewhere?" he sneered.

She could have screamed at her own stupidity. She ought to have known that Maxwell wouldn't have got deep into conversation, leaving her to her own devices, with the boat unattended.

Quite apart from the fact that she had seemed so near to escape, it was frustrating to realize that once again Maxwell would have the last laugh. She remembered how he had let her go before, knowing she was running smack into the arms of his helpers, and his delight in watching her realize the fact.

Andy was small for a man, not much taller than she was herself, and slightly built. She wondered for a reckless moment if she could overpower him and go ahead with her plan to escape. Almost immediately she dismissed the idea as being preposterous. These thin, wiry types often possessed superhuman strength and she suspected that in a clinch of that nature, or any nature, Andy would be cruel.

Almost as if he'd dipped into her mind and taken out the dark thoughts hovering there, his eyes flicked over her in a sensual way that was full of implied meaning, and she shuddered at what might happen if he overcame her. He was watching her intently. She could feel the lecherous probing of his slit eyes even though she had averted her face. The way he looked at her made her feel unclean. If he offered to touch her she didn't know what she would do.

"Thinking of taking a little trip, were you?"

"Yes." There was little point in denying the obvious.

"Back to the mainland?"

"Yes."

"The laird said you came of your own free will."

"Then I want to leave of my own free will."

"You said he was kidnapping you."

"Did I?"

"Know how to handle a boat, do you?"

"What's it to you?"

"I just thought you might need some help."

"Would you help me?"

"I might. He's no right to keep you here if you don't want to stay, even if he is the laird."

She didn't trust him, but what alternative did she have but to enlist his help—if that were possible? She couldn't get it out of her head that he wasn't sincere, that he was playing a macabre game of cat and mouse with her. That he was having a bit of fun at her expense and hadn't the slightest intention of assisting her.

"Will you take me to the mainland, Andy?"

"How badly do you want to go?"

She swallowed tightly. "I'll pay you well. I haven't any money on me now, but I'll make a note of your address and when I get home I'll post it on to you." She silently cursed herself for not having the foresight to bring Glenda's handbag with her. Her bid to escape had been the impulse of a moment's thought. She'd needed to get away quickly, before Maxwell realized what she was doing and before she lost her nerve. It hadn't entered her mind to go upstairs to her bedroom to fetch the handbag, even if she would have dared to waste the extra precious minutes. "I've a tidy sum saved up in the bank. It's yours if you'll help me to get away now."

His head went from side to side in refusal. The hot gleam in his eye sent cold shivers down her spine. "Promises are no good."

"Trust me. I'll send the money."

"I want payment now."

"How can I pay you now? Be reasonable. I've just told you I haven't got any money on me," she said, trying to keep annoyance out of her voice.

"Who said anything about money? Did I? There are other ways to pay. If you set your mind to it I'm sure you'll think of a way that's acceptable to both of us."

"Are you saying what I think you are?" She hoped, forlornly, that she was mistaken in what she thought.

He smiled slyly. "What's good enough for Mr. Ian is good enough for me."

"Forget it!"

She made as though to go, but his arm shot out, barring her way. She tried to duck underneath, but his fingers, long and as powerful as she had dreaded they would be, gripped her by the shoulders.

"Don't tell me you're not missing it! Your man on his back and no telling if he'll be of use to you again."

"Take your hands off me."

She realized that, although he was by no means drunk, he had been drinking—enough to impair his judgment, give him the courage, or the foolhardiness, to step out of line.

She couldn't think where her judgment had been in thinking that he would help her in the first place. He worked for Maxwell. He wasn't going to put his job at

risk by assisting her to escape. Maxwell wouldn't stand
for that. Even if the bargain Andy was making had
been acceptable to her, which it wasn't, he wouldn't
have kept his side of it.

But Maxwell wouldn't condone this, either. Didn't
he know that he was putting his job in jeopardy by
even touching her? His alcohol-laden breath filled her
nostrils, its unevenness telling of his sexual arousal.

"Don't be a fool, Andy. Let me go."

"Mr. Ian's got good taste. All I want is a little kiss.
Surely you can't begrudge me that?"

His lips were slippery against her cheek as she
turned her face away and deflected the kiss from its
intended target.

"You're a bonny wee lassie," he groaned thickly.
"The laird must be half out of his mind, holed up with
you and him with the burden of misplaced loyalty to
that weak brother of his forbidding him to take a bite.
Unless . . . maybe you haven't been missing it at all. A
man's own needs can strain the fiercest loyalty and the
laird's a man, true enough. A fine, virile specimen at
that."

Wave upon wave of distaste and abhorrence
washed through her. She could hardly believe that this
conversation was taking place. The firm hold he had
on her didn't give her a lot of room to maneuver. She
managed to lift her hands to push him away, but he
was quicker that she was and his hands left her
shoulders to catch hold of her wrists. His mouth came
down and this time there was no evading his hot, wet
lips covering hers in a bitter kiss. He let go of her
wrists, but that was no release because he'd got her
back sharply up against the wheel. She hadn't realized
that he had unfastened her coat until she felt his rough
hands pushing up her sweater and touching the bare
flesh of her ribcage.

"Get away from me," she yelled at him, her voice shaking with disgust.

"Be nice to me, bonny lassie, and I'll be nice to you. I'll take you to the mainland."

"I wouldn't trust you to take me anywhere. Be nice to me and let me go. Then *I'll* be nice to *you* by not telling Mr. Ross."

"It will be your word against mine. I've never lied to him. Leastways, I've never been found out," he added, grinning evilly.

Whereas every time she opened her mouth to protest that she wasn't Glenda Channing Maxwell thought she was lying. She was fully aware of Maxwell's low opinion of her.

She decided to change her tactics, play on his vanity. "Why, Andy? Why are you doing this? You're an exceptionally good-looking man. The girls must be queuing up for you. You don't need to take an unwilling woman."

"I don't go short," he said boastfully. "But a man likes a challenge. It's more fun. And there's a bit more icing to you than there is to the lassies I usually go out with."

That hadn't achieved much. The motion of the boat was in her head and a heaving sickness was in her stomach as she renewed her struggle to free herself. She kicked and punched and pummeled, but he was stronger than she was. She knew that although their wild thrashing about was causing the boat to pitch it was too big and sturdy to capsize. But she wished it would. She would rather have an icy ducking than endure this scuffle for much longer. It was like some horrible nightmare, the kind when you're trying to run but your feet are weighted, and in any case there's nowhere to run.

She couldn't believe it when Andy suddenly released her. She stared at him through the wild disorder of her hair, unable to comprehend this new turn of events, incapable of coherent thought.

He was saying something to her, spitting the words out with an urgency that demanded to be obeyed, but it was a moment or two before anything registered in her brain.

"Are you deaf, woman? Straighten yourself, I tell you. It's himself coming."

Did he mean Maxwell? Yes, there he was, his face as black as thunder, taking his anger out on the ground as he strode forward.

She smoothed down her sweater and her hair, then rebuttoned her coat with clumsy fingers that wouldn't move quickly enough for pride's sake. She gave heartfelt thanks that Maxwell had missed her at the house and had come looking for her, but she bemoaned the price she was being made to pay in lost dignity.

Angus was with him, but it was Maxwell's reaction she was most concerned about and which caused her the most pain. His eyes scored over her, taking in every detail of her disheveled appearance and she held her breath in anticipation of the severe dealing that Andy could expect.

Andy was shuffling his feet and there was fear on his face.

Maxwell barely gave Andy a glance, so absorbed was he in looking at her, his keen penetration reading the shame and degradation in her heart. But something was not as it should be. The sympathy that ought to have been there was missing. His contempt flicked over her and she knew that he had drawn the wrong conclusion. He had mistaken her natural feeling of outrage and humiliation at being the innocent party in Andy's little game as guilt and anger at being caught.

As always, where she was concerned, he had
prejudged. His mind was quite made up as to where
the fault lay and whom to blame, and to her dismay
and further frustration, it wasn't Andy.

Andy was quick to sum up the situation and even
quicker to take advantage of it. Before Gemma's eyes
he changed from the lecherous hothead into a bewildered boy who didn't know what was happening to
him or how it had come about.

"I couldn't help myself, Mr. Ross, sir," he sniveled.
"She egged me on. She said she thought I was an
exceptionally good-looking man and that the girls
must be queuing for me."

Maxwell turned to Gemma. "Did you say that?" he
asked curtly.

"Yes, but not in the way—"

"Andy?"

"She said that if I was nice to her she'd be nice to
me," Andy replied, letting his eyes drop painfully
away from Maxwell's at just the right moment. How
touchingly ashamed he looked, how wronged.

"I won't ask what Miss Channing meant by being
nice to you, Andy. It's better left unsaid. What—" he
paused deliberately—"service were you asked to per-
form in return?" Maxwell inquired, grim-mouthed.

"She wanted me to take her to the mainland, sir."

Maxwell's eyes swung round to fix on Gemma.
"What have you to say to that?" he demanded, his
countenance harsh, his mind closed to her even as he
invited her to speak in her own defense.

This was the ultimate injustice. It was patently
obvious that he wasn't going to believe her, that his
sympathies were with Andy, who was giving an Oscar-
winning performance of a green country boy.

"You know what I've got to say," she replied hotly,
bristling with indignation. He was so quick to con-

demn her that he asked to be taken in. "Of course I tried to get Andy to take me to the mainland. But all I offered in return was money."

"Where is it?" he demanded, his assumed patience and silky sarcasm setting her teeth on edge.

"Where is what?"

"The money you offered him. Did he pocket it?"

"I didn't have any money to give him."

"I see."

"Not on me. I was going to send it to him later."

She was fuming and all too aware of the triumphant smirk on Andy's mouth. She cast a fleeting glance at Angus to gauge his reaction, but all that was apparent was his acute embarrassment at being forced to witness this sordid scene. This increased her fury. Wasn't it enough that she had suffered at the hands of that sex-obsessed beast? Did Maxwell have to humiliate her in front of Angus, whom she liked and whose good opinion mattered to her?

"You never see anything because you never listen to what I say," she accused. "You're consistent in that you always condemn me without a hearing. You made up your mind at the beginning about me, about who you think I am, and you're too damned bigoted, too high and mighty to concede that you just might have made a mistake. The infallible Maxwell Robert Bruce Ross doesn't make mistakes; he's much too superior and so I must be lying. Oh, what's the use?" she said, sweeping her hands in a gesture that conveyed the futility of going on. "You'll believe anyone but me. You're easy to convince because you want to think the worst of me. The dice were loaded against me from the start. Believe it if you want to! Believe that I enticed Andy and offered my body to him as a bribe! I j-just don't care."

The break in her voice threatened to take her into

pathos. That would have been too horrible to bear and she desperately sought to control this weakness by digging her fingernails into the palms of her hands to stop their tell-tale trembling and swallowing deeply to keep her voice steady. At the same time she was conscious of the fact that Angus was staring at her open-mouthed. Even Andy's pleased smirk had been swallowed in a comic grimace of surprise. Perhaps they'd never before heard anyone speak up to Maxwell, Laird of Glenross, in this way. As if to confirm that thought, they both looked to Maxwell, transparently waiting to see how he was going to answer the attack.

They were not by themselves. Gemma was beginning to wonder if she'd been quite wise to tell Maxwell off in front of his employees. She bit her lip and waited in trepidation to see how she was going to be punished.

In the heavy silence that came down like a blanket of condemnation she worked it out in her mind that Maxwell was deliberately refraining from speaking in order to unnerve her. What was more, he was succeeding. It needed very little to tip the balance of her control, which was on the slide anyway. She must not let him disconcert her, make her fall still deeper into disgrace. Too much injustice had been done to her as it was. She didn't know how she was going to manage it, but she must not let him reduce her to tears.

Just when she thought her nerves couldn't stand it a moment longer he spoke, delivering an icy command that was as sharp as a rap across the knuckles. "Get off that boat and up to the house. I'll talk to you later."

Gemma was in no hurry to get off the boat. The small strip of water that separated them offered at least an illusion of protection. Ashamed of that small flash of cowardice, feeling that she had taken about as much as she could stand, she threw the last remnants of caution to the wind. She would not submit to his domination.

"No!" Defiance flamed in her eyes and on her cheeks. "I will not be sent away like this. I am the innocent party. Andy jumped on *me!* I didn't offer him the kind of inducement you're suggesting. If you hadn't come along just when you did I cringe to think what would have happened. But it certainly would not have been at my invitation."

She was not the only one astounded by her temerity. Once again there was a breath-held silence with Andy listening avidly and Angus making an awkward pretense of interest in the rope mooring the boat, the anxiety on his kind face spelling out all too clearly to her that her previous fear was justified and that no one defied Maxwell Ross and got away with it.

The dark olive eyes stared icily into hers for a long moment and then he repeated the command. "Get off that boat and up to the house."

He put his hand out to help her ashore. She glared at it resentfully, all motion held in check by impotent anger. Fearing the consequences of continuing to defy him, she took the only option open to her. She put out her hand, accepted his assistance, and then walked toward the house, her back stiff with mortification that in the end she'd had to submit to his mastery.

5

~~~~~~~~~~~~~~~~~~~~~~

She had backed down, but in all fairness, what else could she have done? In fairness to Angus, whose embarrassment had shown a possible leaning to her, but set against this were his years of loyalty to his employer, which were too strong to be ignored. To keep up the confrontation would have increased his discomfort. And in fairness to herself, because in his quietly cold, enviably controlled way, Maxwell had looked determined enough to remove her from the boat by physical force if necessary, and she had suffered all the indignity she could take for one day without that. A lifetime's indignity had taken place in the space of an hour.

She let herself into the house by the back door. She sat at the kitchen table, her head in her hands. She hated all men. She especially hated Maxwell for taking Andy's word against hers and she really, if stupidly, hadn't expected that. She hated Andy for daring to touch her. Perhaps all he had intended was a kiss and a grab and it wouldn't have gone any further, but she couldn't be sure. He had touched her and she felt soiled because of it. There was a dull, sick feeling in her stomach and she knew it would be a long time before she could forget the horror of being trapped in his arms.

She was still sitting there when Maxwell came in. She straightened up, expelling her breath in a long, shuddering sigh as she cast him a wary look.

The bruised eyes in the haunted little face received no compassion; his expression reviled her for all the things he thought she was, for what he believed she had done to his brother and to a lesser degree for leading Andy on.

She flattened her hands against her head, trying to contain the disarray of her hair, wishing she'd thought to tidy it instead of wallowing in confusion and despair. It was bad enough to be regarded as a tramp; she didn't have to look the part.

She wished now that she'd made herself scarce before he came in, gone upstairs to her bedroom or busied herself with some household chore. Anything not to have to talk about what had happened. She was too vulnerable and too near the tears that must not be shed at all costs.

There were menace and purpose in his every step as he crossed the room. Towering above her, he lifted her face with one curved forefinger. "I hope you are satisfied."

"Satisfied?"

"I fired Andy. That's what you wanted, isn't it?"

Her spirits soared, putting the glow back in her eyes. "No, it isn't what I wanted. I'm not that vindictive. I just wanted you to believe me. I'm not gloating because you've forced Andy to leave; I'm just happy that you believe me."

The cynicism on his face dashed her hopes. "What put that into your head?" His eyes drilled into hers. "You asked for what you got. Andy's a mere boy, used to uncomplicated, straight-dealing girls. He was out of his league with you. I'm sure you're capable of distracting a much stronger character from the dull path of duty, so what chance did he have? You'd go to any man's head."

The pressure of his finger on her chin increased, as if he was working some vengeance out of his system. The way he'd said, "You'd go to any man's head," gave her the strangest feeling that this touched him personally and had nothing to do with either his brother or Andy. She didn't think he'd meant to say that. He had spoken his thoughts out loud. Did she go to *his* head? Was he having difficulty keeping his own emotions in check? It didn't seem possible for her to be so electrically aware of him as a man and for him to feel nothing in return. It was more probable that he was generating some of the heat, that the intense current was flowing from one to the other, a two-way thing. Even now, as her mind ran to fervent conjecture, the sensual pressure of his touch on her chin was sending abrasive shock waves, shafts of fire, through her entire system.

His hand dropped away with shattering, telling abruptness. Thumb and forefinger were rubbed agitatedly together, as if he was trying to rid the intensity of feeling that was burning there. The tension was such that she thought if it didn't ease, if the atmosphere between them didn't find a more relaxing level, something would snap, like a tautly held piece of elastic that just needed one final twist to fragment.

"If you think I'm to blame for the way Andy acted,"

she said gruffly, her voice gaining more composure as she went on, "why did you fire him?"

"He had whisky on his breath. On his own time, providing it doesn't interfere with his work the next day, he can drink himself insensible for all I care. I won't have him drinking on my time."

Was that the only reason? she wondered. "Isn't dismissal harsh treatment for a drinking offense?"

"If it were the first time, perhaps. It wasn't. I've had to reprimand him about this twice before. I warned him that if it happened again I would send him packing."

"I see."

"Don't tell me you're regretting your part?"

"My part!" she said in rising indignation. "I'll tell you what my part amounts to. If I hadn't skipped out of the house with the intention of trying to take the boat you wouldn't have followed and I don't suppose you would have had cause to talk to Andy and you wouldn't have known that he'd been drinking."

"You could be right about that."

"I'm glad I'm right about something. It makes a change. As far as Andy is concerned, in one way I'm sorry he's got the sack because I don't like to hear of anyone losing their livelihood, and especially not because of me."

"Don't burden your conscience on that score. You'll observe that I'm giving you the benefit of the doubt and assuming that somewhere in that self-centered and conniving little head of yours there is a conscience. Andy got the push because he took a dram too many. If it hadn't happened today it would have happened at some later date."

"Don't get me wrong. I feel as though it's through me, even though I'm no way to blame, but I'm certainly not sorry that I won't have to see him again. I wish I'd never got involved."

She was aware of the disdain in his eyes and hated him for it.

"You should regard this as a lesson, then. In the future, only seduce men who can take it."

"That's the most preposterous, unfounded accusation you've thrown at me yet. I *did not* seduce Andy. I asked him if he would take me over to the mainland. He strung me along that he might, and then he made a grab for me. Something like that couldn't happen to you, more's the pity, and you don't seem to possess the compassion to know that it isn't a very pleasant experience."

"Come on. Andy wouldn't have dared to lay a finger on you if you hadn't made an offer."

"Believe what you want. You always do. When I said I wished I'd never got involved I didn't mean just over this. I meant right from the beginning."

"I imagine that Ian does, too."

"I've never met Ian." She might as well not have spoken.

"You bewitched him. If he hadn't fallen for those wide, melting eyes and that beguilingly pure and angelic little face he would have got round to marrying Fiona and he wouldn't be where he is now."

"Got round to marrying Fiona?" she said, jumping on that, her brow crinkling on the cold tone in which he spoke. "That sounds a negative approach to marriage. I might even risk a calculated guess that in considering it Ian would have been bending to family pressure."

"Fiona would have been a sensible match for Ian. She's sweet and affectionate, with a keen sense of loyalty and moral responsibility and she keeps her nose clean. Ian should have had his head examined for preferring a packet of trouble like you."

"Why bother about Ian?" she flashed at him. "Why be so altruistic as to let your brother pick this peach of a girl from under your nose? Why don't you marry her yourself?"

"I could do worse."

"Huh! It wouldn't do for me. I can see it all so clearly. Your perfectly laundered socks would always be in matched pairs, your slippers warming by the fire, your favorite meals cooked to perfection, no hint of extravagance and little wifey falling into a faint if another man so much as looked at her. So tediously predictable." She raked her hand through her hair, as if by doing so she could bring the words she was searching for out of her head. "Believe me, I'm not scoffing at those qualities in a marriage, just as long as they're not the reason for getting married in the first place."

"Interesting. What would your reason be for getting married?"

"That's easily answered. Sense wouldn't come into it. I'd love him insensibly. And I'd consent to marry him only if I couldn't bear *not* to marry him. It wouldn't matter if our characters were poles apart if we were compatible in other areas. I'm not denying that it's nice when everything is comfy and a bonus when it's wrapped up in family approval, but sometimes it seems to me that a few obstacles along the way can forge a stronger partnership. There could be no danger that you had drifted into it because it makes a tidy arrangement." For some reason not quite known to her, perhaps because she was vexed by his rock-solidness and inflexibility, she slid him a flirtatious look from under her lashes. "You wouldn't enter into marriage with Fiona, or anyone for that matter, to please your family. You'd marry to please one person only—*yourself.*" Her tongue rested on this last word with savage emphasis.

"I would also please one other person—the fortunate girl I married. I would give pleasure as well as take it. The more I took, the more I would give."

Furious with herself for being the one to introduce that sensuous note, she lashed out tautly. "Does everything have to come down to sex?"

"Have I misunderstood something? I thought I was agreeing with you. Didn't you say that if the other areas were all right—and by 'other areas' I took it that you meant sexual compatibility—things like friendship, shared interests and having temperaments that complement and don't clash weren't all that important?"

Had she really said that? Yes, she supposed she had. He had merely brought her words into sharper focus and given them more punch. She sighed. He was getting her confused. Moreover, it was not in her nature to maintain a quarrel and she felt she had been drawn into this one against her better judgment. She had been manipulated into saying what she had by his manner. It had taunted her to try to provoke a reaction in him and, instead, he had turned the tables on her by inviting her reckless comments. She always seemed to be in the unenviable position of backing down. Be damned with caution, and the consequences, too! This time she would not back down.

With a lift of her chin and a significant sparkle in her eye she said, "There are many kinds of love. The affinity you have for a parent, a brother, a sister or a favorite relative. The tender love you feel for a helpless creature, a child or an animal. The love you have for a work of art, a piece of sculpture or a painting, and for growing things, trees and flowers and all the beauty of the earth and sky. But most important of all, perhaps the reason for our existence, is the love that's strong enough for you to give yourself to one person in a marriage which you hope will last for the rest of your life. That's some love; it's got to be to match up to such a huge commitment. The most precious love of all and, because of its intimate nature, the most physical. That side's got to be all right, otherwise the whole structure will fall down. And if it is, if you feel that intensely about someone, how can love *not* follow?''

"What if the fascination doesn't last? What if the chemistry burns itself out like a meteorite?''

"I don't know. It's a risk I would have to take."

She heard him laugh and the laugh was the perfect partner to the cold and humorless smile on his lips, heard it and took an involuntary step back because she knew what it masked. She knew what he was thinking, knew it as surely as if he had placed his lips on hers to prove the point. Their chemistry was right. It took only a look to send shock waves down to her toes, but under no circumstances would she marry him.

He was playing with her, she realized wretchedly. He had put words in her mouth and now he was putting unnecessary fear in her heart because he was only looking, employing eye-play to make her admit to the attraction that leaped between them like a living flame. The fascination she felt for him was the devil's doing, poles apart from love, and would always remain so. She could never love him. Never. It would make nonsense of everything she had said.

She lowered her eyes, conceding victory to him.

Perhaps he didn't realize that, or didn't want to. That kiss on the quayside, administered to prevent her from crying out for help, had a lot to answer for. It had stirred things between them. If he had been looking for an excuse to repeat it she had given it to him by airing her views and he wasn't going to have it snatched back until he'd taken advantage of it.

His arms came out to her and she allowed herself to be pulled into them like someone in a trance. She went forward with a puppet's compulsion, but also with a puppet's jerkiness and non-involvement, showing neither resistance nor willingness. Even in her mesmerized state she knew that it was the expression on his face which held her aloof. His pupils were dilated, indicating arousal, but his eyes also showed scorn and bitter contempt. She didn't know which of them he hated more, and all because of his wrongful assumption that she belonged to his brother. Himself for desiring her, or her for being so wantonly free and not thrusting him off?

In a sense they were both putting things to the test. He was intent on making her eat her words and she was finding out if she could blank out the memory of Andy. She had read somewhere that the most common cause of coldness in a woman was an unhappy experience. Luckily for her things hadn't gone beyond horseplay, but her revulsion had outstripped the deed. She had wondered if she could be in a man's arms again and not feel a recurrence of that emotional upheaval.

It was a relief to feel stirrings within her, to respond in warmth, to acknowledge the pangs of sweetness running through her like melting honey and wallow in the joy of knowing that something wonderful hadn't been spoiled for her. She was grateful to Maxwell for taking this lurking fear from her and perhaps that was why she gave her lips to him so readily. Yet she did not lose herself so totally in that kiss as to be unaware of the danger she was inviting, the risk she was taking in permitting familiarity with a man while being in his care. She knew that Maxwell would not force her into anything, but that in no way wiped out the danger, because he would never have to force his attentions on a woman. The touch of his lips, so gentle on hers, was a powerful persuasion, insuring his welcome.

She was divided by the emotions she felt and the ones she knew she ought to feel. She was a traitor to herself, a disgrace to her sex to enjoy the advances made by someone who thought so ill of her. The confusion of her thoughts was intensified by the fact that it was Glenda he hated, but not Glenda he held in his arms.

She wasn't in his arms under false colors. It wasn't anything in Glenda that was invading his senses and drawing him to her. He might have Glenda's name on his lips, but the lips that were tormenting him to frenzy were hers. It was Gemma Coleridge he was so strongly attracted to that he was losing track of reason.

"What is it about you?" he despaired huskily.

"Maxwell." His name was gentle on her breath and then his mouth swooped again, drawing her back into the dangerous excitement.

Time, place, nothing mattered except desire. Desire burning on their lips and tingling along their nerve-ends, holding them enraptured in fascination's spell. There wasn't a thing she could do to hold aloof from it. One moment she was on relatively safe ground and the next she was hurtling into a vortex of passion. Their mouths, his firm and demanding, hers subservient to the sensuality of his, clung and parted and clung again. Passion without compassion as the bruising exploration claimed not only the obedience of her lips but compelled every part of her body to yield to him.

With a sigh of resignation her hands lifted to link submissively round his neck, an action which brought her body close to his. His splayed hand on the small of her back brought her closer still, and with that the awareness of his masculine response and the disturbing realization that it was not unpleasant to her.

A weakness attacked her limbs, making her his slave. Instead of raising barriers against him, which she ought to have done, she found herself rising on tiptoe to get nearer to him. His tongue trailed down her cheek. His free hand went to her neck, caressing its white column before moving down over her sweater. Her breasts firmed in tingling anticipation as his hand hovered and she knew the meaning of frustration in the endless moments before his fingers molded to her shape. Her thick, chunky sweater was an obstruction and she made no protest as he pushed it up out of the way to stroke the swell above the satin and lace cups of her bra. She didn't even offer to evade his hands when, having dealt with the fastening, he removed even the intrusion of that dainty covering. Her breath rose and fell with such alarming rapidity that she wondered if her heart could take it even as she delighted at the intimate abrasions of his firm but surprisingly gentle fingers.

When his head bent so that he could take the rosy tips of her breasts into his mouth, each in turn, she gasped aloud in shock. The warmth of his mouth was entrancing, hypnotic. Her nipples swelled as the blood coursed like fire through her veins and when he took one between his teeth and nipped gently she shuddered with unwilling arousal.

So caught up was she in the heady sensations running through her that she hardly noticed when his hand strayed to the waistband of her jeans, undid the snap, and slipped inside. The thin fabric of her panties was the only barrier between his caressing fingers and her soft, moist womanhood and she groaned as one finger dipped quickly beneath the elastic and teased her gently. With small, circular, tormenting motions he brought her tremblingly against him, assailed above and below by a dangerous excitement she could not combat. Just when she thought she could stand no more he raised his head and his hand ceased its delicate play. She couldn't be sure but she thought she actually moaned in regret when his hand dropped away. It was such an anticlimax. She knew from the expressions crossing his face that she was not the only one in turmoil. Horror, pain, and contempt followed each other in rapid succession as his eyes held hers until, her cheeks glowing with embarrassment, feeling shame where none should exist, she tilted her chin at him in blazing fury. Yet even as his icy glance raked over her she knew that it was Glenda Channing his conscience had made him push away; his body wanted Gemma Coleridge back in his arms, her face pressed close to his heart's aroused, clamorous beat.

Why wouldn't he listen to her? She wasn't his brother's property and he had no cause to feel guilty or make her feel disloyal.

"I'm my own woman," she shrilled in anger. "No one, not your brother nor any other man, has a claim on me. I wear no rings on my fingers." She waved them under his nose. "I've promised myself to no one; I'm as free as the air."

"Free?" he queried, his voice sneering but his face impassive. Only a working muscle in his cheek betrayed the strain of keeping up the front he was putting on. Having seen the explosion of his anger once, when she'd brought Barry's name into the conversation and he'd flown into a demented rage at the thought that she might have slept with him, she was sure that it was only a front, that fire and violence were locked none too securely beneath the ice. "I don't know about your being free," he drawled sarcastically. "I do know that you're cheap."

Anger rose in her, sending the blood rushing through her veins. She had a sudden urge to lash out at him, but as she couldn't match up to him physically she controlled her itching fingers and attacked him verbally. "I didn't make the first move, remember? Don't make me a scapegoat for your conscience, if that's what's troubling you. You were pretty quiet on the subject of brotherly loyalty a minute ago. It was convenient to forget a lot of things while you were having your fun."

His mouth compressed in a way that had her biting her lip and bitterly regretting her outspokenness. She would have regretted making that passing reference to his brother in any case, even without fear of reprisal, because her anger wasn't really the malicious kind. She knew how desperately worried he was about his brother's condition and she didn't want to add to his burden.

"I'm sorry," she said quickly. "That was hitting below the belt. It wasn't even true."

"On the contrary, it was a fair comment. I did forget a lot of things I should have remembered. I also made the first move. But that doesn't absolve you from all blame. You'd make a saint go off the straight and narrow, and I've never professed to be a saint. I'll admit that my judgment has taken a knock."

"That's magnanimous of you," she scoffed.

His mouth tightened. "I was aware of how you charmed my brother half out of his mind. From the moment he first met you he talked of no one else and acted like a besotted boy. I would have been amused by it all if it hadn't been so pitiful. I thought he was showing a weakness of character, being unduly susceptible to allow himself to get into that state over a woman. Poor Ian, I see I've been hard on him. He didn't stand a chance. I completely underestimated you. I had no idea you were such a danger to mankind. I should have realized when Andy—your most recent conquest—took a tumble for you."

"I thought *you* were my most recent conquest," she couldn't resist flinging at him, bridling at his sarcasm and arrogance.

His eyebrows rose derisively. "My apologies for touching you. I did enjoy the experience; you know how to please a man. But I can promise you that it won't happen again."

How dare he be so insulting! "Thank you. I'm delighted to hear it."

"Have a care," he warned. "My patience isn't unlimited and neither is the amount of rope I'm prepared to give you. As I was saying, there won't be a repeat. You can look as beguiling as you wish if it pleases you to keep in practice. I'm up to all your tricks. You can look at me from under your lashes and flaunt your luscious body at me, but I'm not buying."

She did look up from under her lashes, she realized, but not in a coquettish way, as he was suggesting, but only when she was shy or unsure of her ground. As for the other accusation, she did not flaunt herself. "My body is not for sale."

"And I wouldn't have it as a gift."

She was too emotionally overwrought to answer that outrage. Anger and tears vied for first place. The former had proved to be a useless weapon against him, making not the slightest dent in his composure, and she'd long since decided that the latter were unthinkable. She would not break down and weep in front of him no matter how much effort it took to control the weakness.

She didn't realize that she was looking at him from under her lashes again until her grabbed her by the arms in a demonstration of icy fury and commanded, "Don't do that. You don't have to prove anything. I've already admitted that your powers to attract a man are immense, but now that I've got your measure they won't work. I can put up a strong line of resistance."

"So you have nothing to worry about!" she retorted, thinking how unfair it all was. She dropped her eyelids so he wouldn't see the tears that were gathering in her eyes. "You're hurting me." The hard fingers bruising her flesh were nothing to the inner pain, but her emotions were getting more and more difficult to hide and she would rather he thought she was wincing from physical hurt than mental torture.

He released his hold immediately, looking taken aback, as if he hadn't realized he was using violence on her. He made no apology; neither was there any intimation of it in his eyes. Just cold condemnation.

"Don't look at me like that," she said.

"Like what?"

"As if I've committed some deadly sin."

"That's only because I acted to prevent it."

"Prevent it?" she said, perplexed. "You mean because you had the willpower to stop just now? No matter how far that had gone it wouldn't have been a sin against your brother."

"Come off it, Glenda. You know that's not what I'm talking about. You know what I mean."

"I'm not Glenda, so I don't know what you mean."

"Aren't you being a little ridiculous in keeping up the subterfuge?"

"It isn't a subterfuge. I mean nothing to your brother and he means nothing to me."

"That's true, whatever else is false. I know he means nothing to you. You've not even troubled to ask about him. My God, but you're hard. A stone would have more feelings."

"I have feelings," she declared passionately. "I'm sorry about your brother. I should have said something, I know that, and I'm sorry about that, too. But it wasn't through lack of compassion. I'd be saddened to hear of any stranger being dragged from the mangled wreckage of a car. And that's what your brother is to me—a stranger."

"You've slipped up badly there, Glenda. But before I go into that I must compliment you on your acting ability. You almost had me believing that you were telling the truth for a minute there."

"I *am* telling the truth," she said wearily, trying not to let his bitterness and contempt get her down, knowing she was getting the backlash of the concern and anxiety he felt for his brother.

"Perhaps you'd care to tell me how you know that Ian was involved in a road accident, then? I most certainly didn't go into the details."

"Angus told me. You've been too busy accusing me of things I know nothing about, condemning me out of hand without a hearing, to tell me anything. I've had to piece the story together in dribs and drabs."

"Oh, really!"

Setting her jaw, she continued. "This is what I've

got so far. The wedding date was set, but then Ian was involved in a serious accident, as a result of which he's in hospital on the danger list, and if he lives there's no guarantee that he'll ever walk again. His fiancée decided that she couldn't bear the thought of spending the rest of her life with—and I'm sorry I've got to word this so cruelly—with a cripple. So she wrote to Ian, breaking off the engagement, a letter which you intercepted. I think it's lucky that you did. There's no knowing what it might have done to him; a bombshell like that shouldn't be delivered until he's strong enough to take it. Believe it or not, I admire you for what you're trying to do. Ian's got enough to contend with at the moment and I think it's noble of you to take the law into your own hands to spare him further heartache and disillusion. As far as I can see, there's only one thing wrong with your plan, and that's picking me up instead of Glenda."

"Not again."

"Yes—but for the last time. I intend to have my say and after this, I promise you, never again. I got this cockeyed notion of taking the boat out and trying to escape to help you. It was in my mind to go to Glenda and plead with her to see Ian through this black patch. She must have loved him once to have agreed to marry him, so I had every hope of convincing her to stand by him now, while he's so desperately ill. Then, later, when he's more able to bear up, she could please herself. It would be odds on that her indifference would show through by that time—I should imagine that sort of thing is difficult to hide—and Ian might want to get rid of her. That's what I hoped to do, but it didn't work out. I tried and failed. It's on your conscience now. When you present me at Ian's bedside, which is presumably what you intend to do the moment he's well enough to know his visitors, he's going to think his mind is affected, or yours, when, instead of his loving fiancée, he sees me."

"Have you finished?"

"Quite finished. Of course you won't believe a word I've said. I didn't expect you to. You're a self-opinionated, pompous bigot who can't conceive the possibility that—just for once—you might be wrong."

6

On legs that were undeniably shaky, she walked out of the kitchen and up the stairs. Once she reached the privacy of her bedroom she collapsed on the four-poster. The down-filled quilt billowed up in protest at the weight of her body and soaked up the tears that flowed unchecked from her eyes.

She could hardly believe that she had spoken to Maxwell like that. If that outburst hadn't convinced him, nothing would. But not one glimmer of belief had softened the awesome look on his forbidding face. Despite the granite squareness of his chin she had thought that if she chipped away long enough she would eventually get through to him, but now she finally accepted defeat. She had meant what she'd said. Enough was enough and she was definitely calling a halt. She'd told him repeatedly that she was Gemma Coleridge without making the smallest impression on him. No one could say she hadn't tried or

blame her for giving up. Let him go on thinking she
was Glenda Channing. It was nothing to her if his poor
brother got the shock of his life at having a strange girl
foisted on him as his fiancée!

Who was she trying to convince? Of course she
didn't mean it. Ian had suffered enough without that
and she couldn't possibly take that hard-hearted
attitude, but what could she do to make things right?
How could she get Maxwell to believe that she was
telling the truth?

Too many things had been against her from the
start. She had been driving Glenda's car and carrying
Glenda's handbag. Coincidence? Or had it been a
deliberate plant? Maxwell had never once wavered in
his version, which was that he had been on the
Ash-le-dale road waiting for her, that is, waiting for
Glenda, by prearrangement. Could it be true? Had
Glenda said that she would meet him and then
changed her mind? He had admitted that he hadn't
met Glenda before, so the arrangements must have
been made by letter or telephone.

When they'd talked in the cafe it had been obvious
to Gemma that Glenda was deeply distressed about
something. She had even asked if talking about it
would help. Glenda's reply had been along the lines
of, "It's all been talked out and decided upon, but not
by me." And then, if Gemma's memory served her
correctly, she'd said, "I shall very probably take the
course I've been told I must take, but that's not the
point. It should be my decision."

At the time Gemma had assumed that her father
had been laying down the law about something.
Clifford Channing would certainly try to talk his
daughter out of entering into a marriage with a partner
who was not in peak physical condition. What if
Maxwell had offered to help her go into hiding to

escape her father's persuasion, but then Glenda had
had a change of heart about going with Maxwell?
Perhaps she knew how intensely Maxwell felt and
what lengths he was prepared to take to safeguard his
brother's peace of mind and so, rather than meet him
to tell him she was backing out, she had hatched this
plot for Gemma to be there in her place. Perhaps she
had been afraid that he wouldn't *let* her back out.
Perhaps the whole idea of planting a substitute had
come to her as she had overtaken Gemma on the
road into Ashford. She could have watched her park
her Mini in the square, then taken her own car to the
garage, where she'd left it in the forecourt before
going in search of Gemma. Ashford wasn't all that big
and even if she hadn't spotted her in Betty's Cafe she
could have made her way back to the square and
waited for Gemma to return for her car. There had
been nothing wrong with Glenda's car, of course, and
her urgent need of transport had been a pretext, all
part of the plot to get Gemma to change cars and then
be picked up in her place. The more Gemma thought
about it the more likely it seemed that she had been
set up. She couldn't get over Glenda's deviousness. If
she was right, then even taking the wrong handbag
had been deliberate on Glenda's part.

What a gullible fool she'd been, tripping over herself
to help Glenda out. Oh, yes, she'd been an easy
victim. How Glenda must have laughed at her willingness to be duped. And could she really blame Maxwell
for the attitude he was taking with all the evidence that
was piled against her?

Angus would be coming again tomorrow to bring
the newspapers. Perhaps there would be something in
one of them about her disappearance. She wouldn't
make the headlines, as Glenda would have done had
she disappeared without a trace, but surely even a

nonentity like herself was worth a couple of lines of space? If she could show Maxwell the report that a girl called Gemma Coleridge was missing from home— the name she had been insisting all this time was hers—then surely he would have to believe her.

She felt better now that she had this tiny hope to cling to, even if it did bring with it the sad reminder that people would be worrying about her. Miss Davies, Barry, her neighbors in the village—if only she could have got word to them that she was all right. Glenda would know, if not her exact whereabouts, pretty much what had happened to her. But having gone to such elaborate measures in the first place, would it suit her purpose to speak up?

Sighing over the problem, seeing no way round it at the present moment, she decided to take a bath and wash her hair, hoping it would soothe her tangled nerves and soak out some of the tension.

Closing the bathroom door, she began to feel sorry for herself because Maxwell hadn't believed that Andy had set the pace and had blamed it on her "immense powers to attract a man." He had called her a danger to mankind. Was she a danger to him? Did *he* find her attractive?

The winsome little face that stared back at her from the bathroom mirror didn't excite her. Milk and roses complexion, that was good, but her mouth was too full and her dove-gray eyes too widely spaced. Her lashes were long and thick and a darker gold than her hair. They swept down and she could no longer see her face in the mirror, nor could she see the shadows her eyelashes cast on her cheeks. Gold-tipped silky cobwebs, demure, yet tantalizing, lifting her face from solemnity into caprice and emphasizing the sensuality of her full, rose-pink mouth.

She ran her bath and, after only a momentary

hesitation, tipped in some of the perfumed, very definitely feminine bath essence she discovered on the bathroom shelf. Morag's or Fiona's? She sniffed. Fiona's, she thought.

She wondered about Fiona, what she was really like and the exact nature of the relationship she shared with Maxwell. Maxwell obviously admired her a great deal—but in what way? Was his affection strictly cousinly and, if so, would it stay that way? Men in Maxwell's position were obliged to marry to produce an heir. What traits would he demand in a wife? She knew the answer to that without even probing for it. All the traits that too-good-to-be-true Fiona possessed!

Her hair said a golden thank you for being washed. If she had one vanity it was her hair. It was long, and in keeping with her self-willed nature, went its own way, which was rather limiting when arranging it. The styles she admired in the glossy magazines were not for her. It either did its own thing, falling in gently bouncing waves to her shoulders, or let her wind it into a height-giving top knot with tendrils that escaped round her face and the nape of her neck. It made her look like a child playing at being grown-up. In the mistaken belief that it made her look older, she put it up now, even though it was still slightly damp. She thought that if she looked more mature on the outside she might feel more confident inside. She needed all the props she could find to handle the delicate situation she found herself in.

Instead of pulling the jeans and sweater back on she thought she'd wear the red housecoat Maxwell had put at her disposal. True to his word, he had dug up something to tie it up with, a rope-type belt which she knotted round her waist, lifting the excess of material to blouse out above it.

The smell of something cooking drifted up from the kitchen, making her realize how hungry she was. It must be something to do with the air, but she had never eaten so much. If she went on like this she feared for her trim waist. Not with too much distress, though, because she was too thin and any extra weight would be welcome.

She paused for a moment at the head of the stairs to look down into the somber reaches of the dimly lit hall. How quickly the days drew in. In a little while it would be completely dark. She deliberately filled her mind with frivolities to shut out the feeling that someone was watching her. Outside, the wind had risen to rush through the Scots pines, making an eerie, whining sound, like the distant skirl of bagpipes. Down in the hall it was unnervingly, chillingly silent. A shadow moved in the murkiness and she tensed, her heart jerking uncomfortably before quickening its beat. Ghosts had a predilection for old houses and Scottish history included more than its share of tormented souls walking down the centuries seeking retribution, carrying feuds beyond the grave.

The shadow moved again and she released her breath in a laugh. It wasn't a ghost that stalked her, freezing her feet immobile and holding her its frightened prey. It was Maxwell. She wondered what had gone through his mind as he stood looking at her, the light behind her making her hair a golden aureole. Why hadn't he spoken to make his presence known?

Afterward she would never know exactly how it happened, what combination of things was responsible. Her unnerved state of mind, the dim lighting, the length of her borrowed housecoat. One moment she was walking down the stairs with confidence, the next her foot was seeking stability where there was none. She tried to regain her balance and she might have achieved it but for the hampering folds of the house-coat. The soft material clung tenaciously to her thighs and wrapped round her legs like a thing suddenly possessed with life and bent on punishing her for having the temerity to wear someone else's property. She couldn't have been more surprised if Fiona had stepped out of the shadows and pushed her down the stairs. She missed three steps to every one she contacted and landed in a heap at Maxwell's feet.

"My God," he said, bending over her, his eyes haggard in his anxious face.

She didn't like to see him looking so worried for nothing. She wanted to tell him that she was all right, but the fall had winded her and although her lips moved no sound came. So she tried to get up. If she couldn't tell him she could show him that no harm had been done. But his hands moved forward to restrain her, supporting and imprisoning her at the same time.

"No," he instructed. "Don't move. I want to find out if anything is broken first."

He unzipped the red housecoat, flung it open and pushed it out of the way. By this time she had got her voice back, and, conscious of the scantiness of her underwear, she started to demur. Her protests were ignored. With a surprisingly gentle touch his fingers ran down her legs, along her collarbone, flattening against her stomach. He eased her arms out of the sleeves of the housecoat and examined each one carefully. There was something expert and clinical in the procedure, but she still found it embarrassing.

"You're very proficient," she said gruffly. "Have you had medical training?"

"Just basic first aid. No bones broken, anyway. That's a blessing, at least." But instead of looking relieved he looked frighteningly grim.

At any moment she expected to be told off for her

carelessness and said, "Please, sir, can I get up now, sir?" in mimicry of a small girl in terror of a disapproving adult.

"I'll carry you."

"But that's not nec——"

Necessary or not, the red housecoat was slung round her shoulders and she was gently lifted into his arms.

In truth, she didn't feel as good as she was trying to make out. She was shaking so much that she couldn't keep still and she was perilously close to tears. It must be the aftereffects of the fall. It couldn't be because she had enjoyed feeling his probing fingers tracing over her body, light yet purposeful, or because he was holding her so close to his chest, as tenderly as if she were a piece of precious china, or because his voice was so kind.

More used to his contempt and disdain, she had no weapons against this new concern and consideration.

He carried her through to the main room, hovering with her still in his arms above the long sofa, showing no apparent hurry to put her down. "I'm sorry," he said, looking into her perplexed eyes.

What was he apologizing for? "What for?"

"For my unbelievable stupidity. I didn't think. I can't imagine what I used for brains. Bringing you to this remote place is the height of irresponsibility. I've cut you off from the world, which was my intention, but I've also cut you off from medical care, should you need it."

"*It's* all right. *I'm* all right. I don't need it."

"Just *be* right. I hope that fall doesn't have unfortunate consequences. That would certainly be bitter irony."

"What would? What do you mean?"

He didn't reply and she looked into his eyes as if she

would find there the answer his lips denied. Black-olive eyes, their expression severely guarded, set in a face held rigid in concern. A carved mask, yet with a very human muscle working in his cheek.

Other emotions began to creep in, as she had known they would. Although his behavior had been circumspect as he examined her, for a revealing moment, just before he'd tucked the housecoat round her shoulders, his eyes had been riveted on her body. She would need to be blind not to see the admiration and desire in their dark depths.

His eyes slid down her body now and she didn't need extrasensory perception to know that he was mentally stripping her of the housecoat and seeing her as he had a moment ago, the beige silk cupping her breasts, half revealing them, the daintiness of her one remaining garment emphasizing the pale smoothness of her legs. She could still feel the cherishing lightness of his fingers curving to the vulnerable hollows in her collarbone, the pressure of his hand against her taut-ened stomach muscles.

She knew with absolute certainty that if she hadn't been protected by Glenda's name, if he'd believed she was herself, Gemma Coleridge, he wouldn't have been looking at her with torture in his eyes. They would have been dark, not with the pain of depriva-tion, but with passion. At this very moment his lips would have been bending to hers. Tantalized out of her mind by her own thoughts, her mouth softened into a kissing shape. It glistened, full and sensuous and tempting, though, had she been challenged, she would have severely denied issuing any provocative invitation. She would have been indignant if someone had suggested that, deep down, she didn't count it a blessing that she hadn't been able to convince him of her true identity. Because if he hadn't been bound by loyalty to the brother who hovered between life and death, instead of putting her down on the sofa he would have turned round, still bearing her in his arms, retraced his steps and carried her upstairs.

He settled her on the cushions, plumping them up to give maximum comfort. When she would have put her feet to the floor he uttered a sharp and remonstrative "No!" and ordered her to lie back and rest.

Never had she felt less like resting. How could her body be cool and self-possessed while she was inwardly on fire and seemingly dispossessed of coherent and sensible thought? Such wild imaginings were totally out of character.

"Aren't you being oversolicitous?" she challenged, annoyed with him for making her feel this way. "I had a minor fall, nothing to make a big song and dance about."

"That minor fall could have had—could still have—major repercussions, as you well know," he said, his anger well in evidence. He didn't seem to be as icily calm as usual, but in the circumstances, that conclusion was far from comforting. "That stupid housecoat is to blame," he said.

If you want to put the blame where it rightly belongs, she thought, it was you. I could tell that someone was lurking down there in the hall—you, as it turned out—and it unnerved me. That's why I missed my footing and fell. However, seeing this as fodder for further argument she kept her supposition to herself. She was disinclined to go on because, despite her protests, she was feeling decidedly weak. She thought she might have bumped her head because it was beginning to ache. At the same time she couldn't let the accusation go unchallenged. "Fiona's stupid housecoat," she corrected.

"I thought you were going to take it up."

"I took the other things up, but this defeated me. As the zip comes right down to the hem it wasn't a simple turning-up job. I would have had to take the zip out and sew it in again."

"Are you easily defeated or not a needlewoman?"

"Neither. It does belong to someone else, you know. The skirt and the jeans have seen quite a bit of wear and I took it that Fiona wouldn't mind donating them to a good cause. And if she did I could always take them down again." She had made a mistake, she realized. Her reference to Fiona had been every bit as incendiary as the other remark would have been and she was bang in the middle of the kind of argument she had wanted to avoid. "On the other hand, the housecoat is comparatively new and very smart. Besides being such a complex job, requiring a lot of unpicking, it couldn't be easily altered back again to fit Fiona. Satisfied?"

"It would have been a lot less complicated if you'd been taller."

"I apologize. It was very stupid of me to inherit the genes that govern height—or, in my case, the lack of it—from my mother, who was also unfortunate enough to be on the petite side."

"And whose temper have you inherited? Cool it, or you'll blow a fuse."

Was there any wonder? She felt that she had been judged, most unfavorably, against Fiona, who not only measured up to the elegant length of the housecoat but was presumably an excellent needlewoman into the bargain. Resentment for the unknown girl rose in her, followed by shame that she could be so petty minded.

"I don't care if Fiona is so tall that you have to stand

on a stool to kiss her. And I don't care if she's the best needlewoman in the world. I don't care, do you hear?"

"As you're shouting fit to blast my eardrums, yes, I hear," he said in a contrastingly quiet voice. "Just as a matter of interest, if *I* had to stand on a stool to kiss a woman I shouldn't want to. Any woman that tall would be a freak."

"It might be of interest to you. It's of no interest to me whom you want to kiss."

Did his eyes contest that? He merely said, "I'll see how the food's going."

"I'll help you."

"You stay here."

Sinking back against the cushions she decided that that was one order she was willing to obey. If only she didn't feel so groggy perhaps she'd be able to cope better. Why did normal conversations always seem to develop into passionate scenes between them? Why was everything such a big issue? Or did it all boil down to one issue? Passion that couldn't be vented one way found other outlets.

Why was he standing there looking at her? He had said he was going to see to the food. Why didn't he go and leave her in peace?

Peace? She'd had none since she met him and she doubted that she would ever find it again. And it was all his fault. He was a man of deep emotions; there were no half measures for him. He would love passionately and he would hate passionately. Right at the beginning, when he first brought her here, she had viewed her position with a certain amount of apprehension. He had kissed her and her world had turned upside down, and she was still apprehensive. The threat was still there, a different kind of threat that brought a similar reaction, but with a subtle difference.

Before, the fear had been *in* her heart. Now, as she met the flicker of hungry sensuality in his hard eyes, eyes deliberately hardened against her, the fear was *for* her heart.

The meal he had prepared was simple but delicious. It was the presentation she had difficulty in digesting. He wouldn't let her come to the table, insisting that she keep her feet up, so he set two trays, sitting opposite in a chair he'd pulled nearer. He must have noticed that she was screwing up her eyes because when she put her hand to the pulse beating in her temple he was quick to say, "Headache?"

"A little one." It was now so fierce that it was tearing her apart.

"Light bothering you?"

"No."

Disregarding the lie he set his tray down and crossed the room to flick two switches. One extinguished the bright overhead light, plunging the room into momentary darkness. The other bathed the room in a soft glow cast by three strategically placed lamps.

"Better?"

"Yes."

Before he sat down he said, "Do you like music? The soft soothing-away-headaches kind, I mean."

"Y-yes."

She hoped the gentle background music would ease the snapping tension between them, a tension which she imaginatively likened to the crackle of static electricity.

But when he put on a romantic Chopin record and inquired "Good?" she was too aware of the mocking smile on his lips to permit the relaxing strains entry into her brain. Her brain was too busy screaming out its suspicions. Good food, a tastefully laid tray, soft lights, relaxing music. All the trappings of a seduction.

She knew that her thoughts were being disobedient again, leading down avenues where no prudent girl would venture. This was because she also knew that brotherly loyalty only went so far, and she couldn't forget the look in his eyes earlier, a look she had seen frequent recurrences of since, a look which overstepped all bounds. His manner toward her wasn't tender, but it was definitely solicitous. That, plus all this, reared an alarming question in her mind. What was it leading up to?

She didn't realize how jumpy she was until he spoke and the unexpectedness of it, because he had seemed to be totally absorbed in the music, startled her so much that her tray began to slide. Her bid to hold onto her plate was successful, but her knife and fork got away and went spinning across the carpet.

Maxwell retrieved them, saying, "I'll fetch clean ones."

"Please don't. I'd finished anyway."

"Lost your appetite?" he taunted, resuming his seat. "You're a strange girl. I never know what's going on in your mind."

It's because I know what's going on in your mind that I behave so strangely, she thought, then said sweetly, "What were you saying?"

"About not knowing what's going on in your mind? Or about you being a strange girl?"

He knew very well what she meant. "No, before that."

"You mean what I said that startled you so much that you almost dropped your tray? I said that when Angus brings the boat tomorrow we'll go back to the mainland with him." He'd abandoned his own tray to pick up her knife and fork. He seemed in no hurry to return to it. Instead he rested his elbows on the arms of his chair, making a steeple of his fingers upon which to prop his granite chin. "Your fall just now brought it home to me. This place is too remote. The risks in keeping you here are too great—so it's back to civilization. That's just the opposite of what you expected me to say, isn't it?"

"How could it be? I had no expectations one way or the other."

"I don't believe you."

"That makes a change!"

Ignoring the sarcasm in her voice he said, "You thought I wanted to go to bed with you."

"I thought no such thing," she said, hastily dropping her eyes.

"That is the most provocative, sensual thing I've ever seen."

"What is?"

"The way you hide behind those fantastically long lashes. It's a good trick, but it won't do you any good." Without giving her time to protest that it wasn't a trick he continued in that same sneering tone. "Desirable as you are you don't need to lock your bedroom door against me tonight, or any night for that matter. You're the kind of poison, a poison for which there is no antidote, I can do without."

7

~~~~~~~~~~~~~~~~~~~~~~~~~~~~~

Next morning, even before she opened her eyes, she sensed that something was different. There was a brightness on her eyelids which hadn't been there before. She raised them and the glare made her blink. She shot out of bed and ran to the window. She had drawn back the curtains last night before getting into bed and now, looking out, she gasped in astonishment. A blizzard of snowflakes was falling against the upper part of the window; the lower part was already blocked by the snow piled up on the ledge.

She opened the window, froze in the icy blast of air, pushed the packed snow away, and looked out on the fairy-tale scene before her. It was a strange white world, an unrecognizable landscape, every contour changed beyond belief by the high drifts of snow. Trees took on new dimensions. Those that weren't buried under their unexpected winter coat were bowing under the weight of their burden. As she watched

the pale sun came over the loch, frosting and sparkling
every peak with a rainbow glitter of light. The beauty
of it took her breath away. It was like a picture from a
children's story book that had suddenly come to
life—any moment the Snow Queen would come
sweeping by on her sleigh drawn by six daintily
stepping reindeer.

It was easy to be fanciful when there was no
pressing need to be practical. Back home she would
have been despairing over how she could get to work,
her mind full of visions of impassable roads. Possibly
she would be switching on the radio for the latest
bulletin, shivering at the horrendous reports of the
inevitable spate of accidents, some fatal, listening to
the accounts of abandoned cars causing further haz-
ards to the intrepid motorist, telephone wires down,
and communications systems out of action.

She wondered how Miss Davies was coping. Not
just today, but every day, and whether a temporary
agency had been asked to send someone to help with
the work.

Closing the window with a sigh, she knew that her
delight in the winter scene was self-defeating. It meant
they wouldn't be returning to the mainland today
with Angus as Maxwell had said they would. Angus
wouldn't bring the boat across in this and they were
trapped on the island until conditions improved.

Looking across the breakfast table a little while later
at Maxwell's sullen face she realized he wasn't used to
having his plans thwarted. Having made up his mind
on an immediate return to the mainland he was
furious at nature's intervention. If it hadn't been to her
own disadvantage to be trapped here she could almost
have been glad that he wasn't the power unto himself
he thought he was and that something could get the
better of him.

Despite his ill temper he cosseted her in cotton-wool for the next two days, sweeping aside her insistance that, apart from a bruised shoulder and the odd stiff joint, she hadn't come to any real harm from her fall.

At first his solicitude was amusing, but after a while the constant watch for some seemingly anticipated deterioration in her health became downright irritating. Finally, feeling like a specimen under a microscope, she turned on him. "Lay off, will you? I'm not going to have delayed-action concussion or anything like that. Stop watching me. It's unnerving. Would you like it if you felt that someone was monitoring your every move?"

He grunted, conceding nothing. But after that his surveillance relaxed and so did she, now that she could move around with ease. The freedom of the house was hers. Maxwell gave her permission to wander at will, to dip into the library of books and the vast collection of tapes and records, built up over the years and guaranteed to provide something to suit every taste. He entreated her to use all the facilities available to make her enforced stay more pleasant. She curtailed herself and refrained from prying into drawers and cupboards for reasons prompted only by nosiness. During her explorations she discovered a trunk in one of the upper rooms that was a terrible temptation, especially for someone of Gemma's vivid imagination. It was a very old-fashioned trunk, the kind that's usually handed down from generation to generation, and was probably chock-full of fascinating things, but she left it unopened.

She took over the housekeeping and had no such compunction about delving into the built-in kitchen cupboards and pillaging the shelves. There was plenty of bread in the deep-freeze, but Morag's cake and scones had all been eaten. She knew she could not hope to eclipse Morag, or even to equal her, but she could whip up a light sponge cake. Although she viewed the unfamiliar oven with trepidation, much to her delight the cake came out beautifully, golden brown and springy to the touch. She lifted it carefully from its tin and put it on a wire tray to cool. Later she would split it and fill it with jam from the supply on the pantry shelf.

She was spurred on by her success, wondering what to do next; then a battered cookery book caught her eye. As she lifted it down from its home it fell open at a section that had obviously seen more use than the rest. She turned the pages to find a fund of recipes, many with penciled notes in the margins in beautiful copperplate script. Things like: *This recipe is over a hundred years old and came from my great-grandmother and is given to the children at Hogmanay. Hogmanay is derived from the Norse word for fairy. The festival is very much bound up with superstition, although some prefer to call it tradition.* Or this little gem: *Spread with butter and rowan jelly; best eaten the same day. Not for Duncan with his troublesome indigestion.* Sympathizing with poor Duncan, whoever he was, for being deprived of this mouth-watering if indigestible treat, she read on, *Don't drown the miller.* Presumably a warning not to add too much water to a pastry mixture. Of the humble haggis it informed: *A must for Burns Supper. Carry to the table to the accompaniment of pipe music. Serve with a dram of whiskey to toast the immortal memory of Scotland's ain Rabbie Burns.* But by far the most intriguing message of all was next to a recipe for a rich chocolate cake. *Maxwell's favorite. I always make it for him as a special birthday treat.* When was Maxwell's birthday? she wondered, flicking the pages back to a simple oatmeal biscuit recipe.

They had fallen into the Scottish way of eating a midday dinner and a high tea. They left the dining room closed and either ate at the kitchen table or, and this was now Gemma's favorite way, made it a tray meal, sitting deep in the armchairs. It was pleasant to draw the heavy curtains against the night and toast their toes before a leaping log fire. The fact that she had started baking was received in taciturn Scots fashion. Although Maxwell made no comment, his hand went back several times to the old-fashioned cake stand which Gemma had found in a cupboard. She was flattered that not a crumb was left on his plate.

Sitting across from him one evening, Gemma decided that if she'd described this to anyone a picture of cozy domesticity and companionable harmony would have sprung to mind, a picture which couldn't have been farther from the truth. The freeze was on in the house as well as outside; it had been ever since her unsuccessful bid to escape and the emotional scene that had taken place afterward. Things had gone too far between them—yet not far enough. Sometimes she looked at him and caught a glint in his eye that told her he was regretting that bringing-her-to-heel kiss which had snowballed on him. He hadn't meant it to deepen the way it had, stirring things already on the boil between them, the antagonism melting beneath a surge of longing, a hunger that demanded appeasement in only one way, a hunger denied and therefore more rampant in its demands.

She noticed the way his hands cupped the arms of his chair, an action that seemed to annoy him because he dragged them fiercely away as if the feel of the padded leather contours was too reminiscent of firm rounded flesh. He would crush his fingers together as if crushing the memory from him. He wore an agonized look on his face, but she felt the pain. She felt responsible and she couldn't bear it. Not that she was solely responsible for his brooding preoccupation; Ian was also on his mind.

Her ability to read his moods was startling. She was like a transmitter picking up his thoughts so that she knew when her presence was causing him agony and when he was sad because now that Angus couldn't get through by boat he didn't have a daily account of his brother's condition. For all he knew Ian could be picking up or, and she read the fear of this in his eyes, he might have given up the struggle.

She tried to harden her heart against him, telling herself that he was in the wrong for bringing her here. The latent regret he had shown was only because of the remoteness of the island. He had said nothing about letting her go once they got to the mainland and she was sure that he still intended to take her to see Ian the moment he was up to receiving visitors. Even though his motive was understandable, and to some extent praiseworthy, as the victim it was stupid of her to be in sympathy with him. But she was. She couldn't help herself. Every time she felt that she was steeling herself against him a weakness invaded her mind and she wanted to reach out to him, wrap her arms round him, kiss the mockery from his mouth and take away his suffering.

For herself, the time was passing quite nicely. If she hadn't been concerned for Maxwell and saddened by thoughts of the worry she might be causing back home she could have enjoyed the break, looked upon it as a highlight in a life that had become mundane. Although the vague stirrings had been there before she hadn't been aware just how mundane until she got away. What of any importance had she left behind? Work that was pleasant enough but lacked the ability to fulfill her. A charming little cottage, the cost of which ate deeply into her salary and the upkeep of which took up most of her free time. Dates with Barry that she had come to regard as routine rather than enjoyable. A television serial she had watched conscientiously through to the next but last installment.

Here she was comfortably housed, with any number of diversions at her fingertips. Good food to eat, good books to read, good music to listen to, and the company of a man who intrigued, infuriated, and fascinated her. No television, true. She would have liked to have watched the last installment of that serial because now, unless there was a repeat at some time in the future, she would never know who the murderer was. But, that apart, she wasn't an addict and hardly missed the box.

Outside it snowed, thawed, and froze by turn. Gemma found that by choosing her time and the path she took very carefully she didn't have to be confined indoors. She had always been a good walker and took the wind, the sleet, and the snow in stride. Her sheepskin coat and boots were blissfully warm and she muffled her head in a long scarf of Maxwell's. She enjoyed the sharp crunch of snow beneath her feet and watched out for the hazardous drifts that leveled the land and hid enormous gulleys.

Quite often Maxwell walked with her, with her but apart. An invisible barrier had come down between them which was difficult to penetrate. Sometimes he looked at her as if he hated her and she found herself getting angry with him about that, but she did her best to disguise it. She never discovered whether he walked with her to protect her, because he considered the exercise beneficial or because he shared her enthusiasm for walking. She suspected that it was a combination of all three.

She had hoped that winter had merely cracked its whip in a token warning to show the extent of its power, but instead of getting milder, after a freak thaw, the barometer dropped sharply. The snow was hard-packed and slippery underfoot, and Iola was held in a grip of ice. The small loch froze over. She remembered what Maxwell had told her, on their first walk together, about testing the ice when he was a boy to see if it was safe to skate on. It had been a boyhood memory full of nostalgia and she had felt privileged to share it.

As they paused to look across the frozen expanse only his eyes were turned frontward. She could tell that his thoughts were again digging back into the past.

"Where are the skates now, Maxwell?" she inquired, a speculative look on her face, then answered her own question. "I suppose that when you grew out of them they were thrown away."

"I doubt it. Grandmother was what the English call a horder and the Scots call canny. She saved anything and everything in case it would come in useful at some future date. I've no doubt that my old skates are tucked away upstairs somewhere in a cupboard or a trunk."

"There is a trunk upstairs. A very old one."

"Grandmother's memory trunk. Everything went in there, all the junk and relics of our childhood. It's even possible that a pair of outgrown and outdated skates will have found an honorable burial there. Why the interest?"

"I thought perhaps I'd like to skate."

"No. I forbid it." The change in his manner was dramatic. One moment he seemed almost amenable, certainly pleasant to talk to, and the next he had reverted to being the unapproachable Highland laird whose word was law. It was imprinted across the dark contours of his face; "I will not be disobeyed in this."

"But you did," she challenged.

"I was a boy, remember. A featherweight," he countered with dangerous coldness.

"I'm not that heavy," she replied, but the resolve was slipping from her voice. It seemed to be a pointless argument as she didn't have any skates and so had no chance of disobeying him even if she could have found the strength of mind to stand up to him.

His teeth gritted. He seemed not to have noticed that she had backed down, because he gripped her arms with bruising force, causing her to wince despite the thickness of her coat. "I was young and reckless and wouldn't listen. But you are damn well going to listen. What's more, you are going to heed what I tell you. The loch is fed by an underwater spring, so even when it looks safe there's always a danger. Don't be like me and find out the hard way, by being on the receiving end of an icy ducking. We thought the grownups were just showing their authority, being overcautious when they made it a condition that we were only allowed to skate when one of them was with us."

"Us?"

"Fiona, Ian, and myself, and any other kids who wanted to tag along. Once we desperately wanted to skate. We'd been waiting for days and just when it seemed right everyone was involved with something else and kept passing us from adult to adult. We decided that if no one could be bothered to come with us we'd go by ourselves. There is one part of the loch, over there by that overhang of trees," he said, pointing, "where we knew never to go. I thought that if we kept clear of that we'd be okay. Fiona and Ian were of an age, I was three years older and therefore responsible for them. Fiona was doing a bit of showing off, she really could cut quite a dash on the ice, and I was watching her. Ian shouldn't have been on that side of the loch at all. Apart from the ice being dodgy there, it's where the water is deepest. The ice gave way; Ian went in. He almost drowned. I thought he had drowned, he was so stiff and cold by the time I got him out. After that the loch was out of bounds and, to see that this order was enforced, Grandmother took possession of our skates."

They walked back to the house in brooding silence. Gemma was sorry that she had brought thoughts of Ian to Maxwell's mind.

A full week had passed since Angus had last brought any news and her nerves, as well as his, were stretched to breaking point. Browsing through the books Gemma found a copy of Robert Louis Stevenson's *Treasure Island*. Robert Louis Stevenson was a Scot, she remembered, whose own life, if not quite as adventurous as his books, had been full of travel. But he came back to Scotland long enough to write *Treasure Island*, a book intended to amuse his stepson, but which brought him fame as a writer and had been enchanting boys and girls ever since.

This copy could equally have belonged to Ian, but, just by the feel of it as she touched the binding, she knew that it was Maxwell's. She opened it and found a double reason to rejoice. Not only was her hunch correct that it was Maxwell's book, but the writing on the flyleaf told her that it had been given to him on his ninth birthday. The giver, his grandmother, had thoughtfully put the date in full. By her calculations he would be thirty-one—when? She scrambled to her feet and raced through the house to check with the pretty kitchen calendar. It was as she thought. Maxwell's birthday was tomorrow!

She remembered that penciled message she had come across about Maxwell's favorite chocolate cake, a thoughtful expression on her face. She lifted the cookery book down from the shelf and studied the recipe. The instructions were very detailed and it required only basic ingredients that could be found in the pantry. What had she to lose? She wrapped Morag's voluminous apron round her waist and began to make Maxwell's birthday treat.

She set the kitchen timer and while the cake was baking she searched through various cupboards and drawers, hoping to find a child's paint box, having it in mind to make a birthday card for Maxwell. She found a stiffish piece of paper that was suitable, but no paints. She did, however, find the stubs of several crayons which would do almost as well.

She waited until the chocolate cake was baked and lifted it out of the oven. Then she took the crayons and paper upstairs to her room, where she wouldn't be interrupted while she worked on his birthday card. She wanted to have a stab at drawing the loch, and the window from her room provided as good a view as any.

She looked out for a long time, letting the scene paint itself in her mind, getting the feel of the ice-covered loch, the snow-heavy sky and burdened trees. Then she began. Considering the limited tools at her disposal she was not displeased with her efforts.

With the birthday card burning a hole in her mind, how she contained herself the next day she would never know. To have presented the card before bringing out the cake for his birthday tea would have spoiled the surprise.

The moment finally arrived. "Happy birthday," she called out, pouncing on him as he entered the room.

He looked from the card to the chocolate cake and

back to Gemma's face. "Quite the little sleuth, aren't you?"

It was difficult to know if he was pleased or whether he thought her childish.

"I got the date by reading the inscription in your copy of *Treasure Island.* I'd already found a penciled note in an old cookery book that this cake was a birthday favorite with you."

"That would be Grandmother's handiwork. She considered it too rich for a young stomach, so my intake of it was rationed."

"Obviously you preferred it to the traditional birthday cake with icing and candles."

"I got one of those as well."

"I'll make a note for next time," she said foolishly, thrown off balance by something in his expression she could not identify. She was envious of his total ease as her nerves began to tighten up.

"Next time? You intend to be around for my next birthday?" he teased, his dark eyes on her, causing her heart to thud erratically as she blinked in panic and surprise at his softer tone.

Not that she trusted it. It was benign on the surface, but there was a thread of something underneath she didn't much care for.

Of course she wouldn't be around for his next birthday. They would have parted company long before then. His mistake about her identity would have come to light and they would have no cause to meet again. Before she had the chance to get out words to this effect he had resumed speaking.

"There was something else that I always got on my birthday."

"Oh?"

"A birthday kiss. Which I'm afraid I accepted under sufferance. Kissing, I thought, was just for girls."

"In that case you won't feel deprived if we skip that part of the ceremony now."

"No," he said, coming to stand by her, casting one arm round her shoulders in a light hold. "I would feel deprived. Put it there," he instructed, tapping his cheek with his free hand.

What was going on in his mind? Would he hold his cheek steady while she reached up to give him the kind of circumspect kiss he would have received from his grandmother? Or did he intend something entirely different? If she twisted free of his arm would she be brought back and made to submit? She realized that by hesitating she was making an issue out of something that might be perfectly innocent. It was just remotely possible that he was teasing her without any devious intent. She quickly stretched to brush her lips against his cheek; the hand left her shoulders and she was free to step back.

"There, that wasn't so bad, was it?" he inquired, coming out from under his mask of light pleasantry and dropping into heavy sarcasm.

"No."

She was furious with herself for allowing him to manipulate her into thinking what he had wanted her to think. There was no doubt in her mind that he had deliberately planted the suspicion that he intended to turn a meaningless peck into a moment of high passion. He had been playing with her, showing her that it was possible for him to hold his finger to the flame without getting burned. He had hated it when he lost his cool that time and he had kept his distance ever since. But that hadn't satisfied him. He'd had to prove that he could get into a clinch situation and still resist her. Big deal! She'd never considered herself to be irresistible anyway, so it was an empty victory. At the same time she thought it was cruel of him to have thrown her into frightened suspense like that, leading her on when he'd achieved his object, finding enjoyment in her petrified indecision.

"In answer to a question you put earlier, *no,* I won't be around for your next birthday. I can't get away from you soon enough, and once I do, I hope that I never have to see you again."

"All this because I didn't make a grab for you! Is this the woman scorned act?"

She glared at him, refusing to grant that comment the dignity of an answer, and instead accused, "You are the most arrogant, the most sadistic man I have ever met."

His smile was crusted in ice. "And you are the most beautiful, the most desirable woman I've ever scorned."

8

~eeeeeeeeee.

She had made the cake and the birthday card as a gesture of friendship, with no ulterior motive. He had misinterpreted that just as he did everything else about her and he had thought it was meant as a provocative trick. The way to a man's heart, and all that. Except that he didn't have a heart, or if he did it was so well hidden that she'd never caught a glimpse of it.

No, that wasn't true. A man without a heart wouldn't show such concern for his brother. That was the crux of the matter, his concern for Ian, his determination not to poach.

He might not like her as a person, but the physical attraction between them was strong. Perhaps, all things considered, she ought to be glad that his principles forbade him to steal the girl he thought belonged to his brother. In a straight contest, if she had been Ian's girl and if Ian hadn't been in hospital, she suspected that Maxwell would have shown no such scruples and would have considered it every man for himself. She remembered the violent explosion of feeling that had swept through her at his touch. He had only to look at her from under those dark brows to crack the foundations of a lifetime and when he kissed her . . . It was just too much. She wouldn't have given anything for her chances if he'd decided to make a determined play for her.

If she were honest with herself she had to admit to wanting him as much as he wanted her, but whereas lust was his total motivation there was more to it for her. Even though she hadn't properly analyzed her feelings for him—perhaps she didn't dare because that would make her more vulnerable still—she knew that heady kisses and entwining limbs might satisfy the requirements of an affair, but they wouldn't fulfill her. Moral principles kept intact for twenty-two years couldn't be carelessly cast aside. There had to be a commitment and, strangely enough, she wasn't necessarily thinking of marriage. She couldn't offer her body without a commitment of the heart. It had to be that—or nothing.

She lifted her eyes to meet Maxwell's penetrating gaze. He was holding the birthday card in his hand and it was obvious by his manner that he had just finished looking at it.

His mouth had a wry twist to it and his eyes were cold as he said, "You never cease to amaze me. I've already discovered what a talented actress you are. Now I see that you're no mean artist, either."

"Don't patronize me," she said, her chin tilting.

"I'm not." The glint in his eyes told her that he knew he was getting under her skin and was amused by this, and so the placatory tone sounded false to her ears. "This is really very good. Excellent, in fact. You've exactly captured the mood of the loch."

"It's a very rough sketch, crude by artistic standards. You're being overcomplimentary."

The icy smile remained firmly on his lips. "Fiona used to dabble in this line."

She shrugged, indicating bored disinterest. "I'm sure she was much better at it than I am."

"I was only going to say," he continued, maintaining that irritating tone of forebearance taken to the extreme, "that some of Fiona's sketching equipment might be around somewhere."

"Thank you. With your permission I'll look round and see if I can find anything."

"Try the trunk. It's as good a place to start as any."

She would have liked to go there and then, but he might think she was grasping at any excuse to leave his company. She disliked the smug, anticipatory lift of his eyebrows, as if he expected her to leap from her chair and run.

She would not give him the satisfaction. With deliberate indolence she rested her strained shoulders back against the upholstery and willed the stiffly held muscles of her face to relax. "Thank you. I will . . . tomorrow."

It was one of the most uncomfortable evenings she had ever spent, but she stuck it out to the bitter end. Before getting into bed she sat for a few moments staring out the window at the white blots of snow, a blizzard of dancing dots in the darkness. When would the weather take pity on her and let Angus get through? It was an intolerable situation. She pressed her fingernails into the palms of her hands in frustration and hoped it would be soon.

By morning it had stopped snowing. She looked up at the winter sky and saw chinks of blue, but as the day progressed they were blanked out by the chilling mist that rolled in from the sea. Maxwell would have called it mist, anyway, but to her eyes it had the density of fog.

She went to the top of the house to look for Fiona's sketching materials. The trunk wasn't locked. She smoothed her hands across the satin darkness of wood that belonged to another century before lifting the heavy lid and letting it rest on its own hinges.

She tried not to pry unnecessarily, putting things to one side that she didn't think were for her eyes, although there didn't seem to be anything personal here. Sure enough, she spotted a box containing tubes of paint, an artist's pad and sketching pencils. As she lifted this out something else was revealed. A pair of ice skates. She judged them to be close to her size. She thought about the frozen loch with longing, but then she remembered Maxwell's instructions not to skate there. If she'd thought that he was cracking the whip of authority for its own sake she would have been sorely tempted to disobey his order. But defiance at the risk of personal safety was just not on. So she put the skates back and contented herself with taking just the painting materials.

Next morning there were a lot more blue patches in the sky and the mist had dispersed. She thought she would like to have another go at the loch, but from a different angle. She cleared the breakfast things away and then poked her nose round the door of the main room and told Maxwell that she was going to find something to sketch. She wrapped up warmly and set off. If she could get the outline down she could do the actual painting in the warmth and comfort of the house.

To get a different angle of the loch meant sketching it from another section of the bank. Not only would the opposite side be ideal but it would serve a dual purpose, because she would be able to get the house in as well. But it looked a long way round and the path was steep and possibly hazardous in these conditions.

All traces of yesterday's mist had cleared away and the surface of the loch was a mirror-glare of reflected sunlight. It looked solid enough. She cautiously tested it with one foot, then she stepped forward and put her whole weight on it, bouncing for good measure. No ominous cracks or creaks met her ear. She was at the loch's narrowest point and this was surely a much safer proposition than going round by the uncertain path.

She crossed easily and reached the opposite bank without a mishap, never once feeling the tiniest bit unsafe. She even lifted her arms and enjoyed the exhilaration of sliding. She wondered what Maxwell had made that big fuss about and wished she'd brought the skates she'd found with her so that she could have skimmed across, like the wind, all the way.

She spent a happy hour, possibly longer, sketching. Despite the cold she was so absorbed in her task that she would have liked to have stayed even longer, but she had to get back to prepare the midday meal.

She was only halfway across when yesterday's mist came back. At first it was nothing to worry about, just scarf-like swirls twirling across the loch, eerie rather than frightening. Ghostly gray-white specters forming and dispersing and forming again until suddenly it wrapped all round her. She couldn't see the bank she was heading for; she looked back and discovered she couldn't see the bank she'd left, either. She told herself not to panic. If she walked in a straight line she would be all right. Surely, even without landmarks to guide her, this wouldn't be impossible.

She seemed to be walking a straight course, but she realized that she couldn't be because she had now been walking longer than it took her to cross initially. The fog—by no stretch of the imagination could this be called mist—stole all the normal daytime sounds, birdcalls, the fleeting step of a deer, the chitterings of small woodland animals and the wind shuddering through the trees. The blanketing silence was unnerving.

She called out Maxwell's name, but all that came back to her was the ringing echo of her own voice. Had she said where she was going? No, she had looked round the door and merely informed him that she was going in search of something to sketch. Was this before or after she'd put on her coat and boots? It was difficult to remember, but she thought that it was before, so Maxwell might have assumed that she meant something in the house. Even if he did look out and see that the fog had rolled in he might not realize that she was out in it and wouldn't come looking for her, at least not right away.

She began to walk more quickly, hoping against forlorn hope to stumble upon the bank, but she seemed to go on forever with no awareness of direction. She shouted Maxwell's name at the top of her voice, then she listened, praying for an answer. What she heard intensified her fears instead of taking them away. It was a loud noise, like the report of a gun—or the cracking of ice. A jagged black line appeared round her and she couldn't find a safe footing. The loch was like a conveyor belt and she didn't know where to turn, which step would take her to her destruction.

A voice—Maxwell's—called out, "Glenda!"

Tears, frozen drops of fear in her eyes, melted on her cheeks. Never had she been so delighted to acknowledge that name as her own.

"I'm here, Maxwell."

"Where? Keep calling out. Your voice will guide me to you. Don't stop calling until I get to you."

"Maxwell, no! Let's do it the other way round. You call out and let your voice guide me to you. I'm much lighter than you are. There's every chance that I shall make it. The ice is cracking all around me; it won't stand your weight. You could drown trying to rescue me."

"What are you saying? I can't hear you."

"I'm saying don't come on the ice. Please, Maxwell, don't. It won't stand your weight." She listened for his reply. It didn't come. "Maxwell, why don't you answer me? Answer me, damn you!" What was he playing at? "You must be able to hear me. Where are you?" she demanded, her voice lifting on hysteria.

"I'm here. Right here," he added. As his arms closed round her she knew that he had been able to hear her every word. He had made her keep talking by pretending not to hear until he reached her.

"You crazy man," she sobbed.

"You crazy woman, and a lot more besides, which will have to wait for the time being," he said thickly.

"I've been walking and walking. It's been a nightmare. I must have been going round in circles."

"Later!" he commanded. His voice was harsh, but she knew it was that way for a reason, as his next words confirmed. "Shut up. I need my ears. Do everything I say and don't utter a word."

If anything, now that Maxwell had joined her, one aspect of the situation was much worse. His added weight was a severe detriment, but she knew that she would never have made it without him. She thought it was probably a false sense of security, but now that he was here she felt safe.

Progress was agonizingly slow. When she wanted to

go faster Maxwell made her walk even slower still, often halting altogether so he could listen. Suddenly she felt her feet whirling clear of the ice. She was being rushed through the air and she didn't know what was happening to her until Maxwell, his arms still firmly clamped round her waist, set her down and she was conscious of her feet touching the bank.

She clung to him, unable to speak or move, just grateful to be safely encased in the warmth of his arms. She didn't know how he was managing to hold himself aloof, why he wasn't taking her offered, upturned mouth in a passionate kiss and conveying the agony that had gone through his mind when he discovered she was missing. At her bleakest moment, just before she'd heard his voice, it had flashed through her mind like a revelation that she didn't want to leave this life which had suddenly become doubly precious to her—ever since, in fact, he had entered it.

To recognize feelings of love could be—should be—the most wonderful experience in the world. It could lift you right up to the stars. Or it could be the worst moment and drag you down into the deepest despair you have ever known. It all depended on your loved one's reaction. Maxwell's reaction shattered her. He wasn't a fool. As her hands clasped tightly round his neck, clinging to his strength with an urgency born of the torment and suffering of her recent experience, he *knew* of her need, her caring. Her body shaped to his in a declaration of surrender. She loved him and she didn't care if he knew it. How could he feel nothing in return? How could his face be so cruelly cold toward her, his voice withering her with condemnation instead of sighing in soft gratitude for her safety?

"You little fool. I forbade you to go on the ice."

"You forbade me to skate," she corrected.

Was he angry because he'd received a fright—because, despite all the signs to the contrary he cared? Or because she'd disobeyed him?

"Don't split hairs," he said, his voice as harsh as the hands that pulled her forward, commanding her to move. "Let's get you back to the house and dried out."

The rain-like mist had soaked into her clothes and chilled her through to her bones, but it was his attitude that chilled her heart.

They didn't speak again as he bundled her roughly toward the house, his long stride showing no consideration for her. No sympathy for the ordeal she had been through, not the merest glimmer of human compassion, touched his dark countenance. Would it have hurt for him to unbend just this once?

"I know you're angry with me, and perhaps you have just cause," she admitted. "I made an error of judgment. Is that such a big crime?"

The only acknowledgment that she received was a swift sidelong look and a grunt.

She sighed. "Everything was fine going across. The ice was as solid as a rock and there was no danger; at least, none was apparent. If the mist hadn't come down I would have got back all right and you wouldn't have been any the wiser. But it did, it rolled in on me without warning. I couldn't keep a straight course and somehow I found myself on the part of the loch you said was dangerous. I'm not stupid. I didn't walk there deliberately to thwart you. Why don't you say something?" she shouted, goaded by his silence. "I wasn't to know the mist would come down like that."

"God Almighty! You weren't to know! Where have you been all your life? Any fool knows how quickly these mists come down, and the islands off this coast are particularly prone to this sort of thing. Don't tell me you've never read anything to that effect?"

"Well, I suppose I have, but—"

"You had to find out for yourself. Your sort are a hazard to themselves and a menace to others. I've never before known so much trouble to come in such a small packet."

With that he lifted her off her feet, opened the door with his free hand, banged it shut behind them with a vicious kick of his foot and carried her up the stairs and into her bedroom. She didn't know what he was going to do next; she half expected to be flung down onto the bed, but she wouldn't have been surprised at anything. As it was, the hand clamping her waist stayed there, the one supporting her legs was removed; she slid down along the length of him and felt her feet contact the floor. Even with the bulkiness of their clothes separating them her consciousness of his nearness caused her to shiver alarmingly. She was blue to her lips with cold and hoped he would put it down to that alone.

"Get out of those damp things. I'll fetch some rough towels from the bathroom to get your circulation going."

In a moment he was back, divested of his own coat, but because her fingers were so numb she was still wrestling with the buttons on hers.

"Let me."

She submitted to having her coat removed with childlike docility because there was nothing else she could do. He took her hands in his, chafing her fingers to bring the circulation back. Then he flattened them against his chest, trapping them there with his own hands. The warmth of his body forced life back into her dead fingers which knew an absurd longing to mold to the hard contours, bury themselves beneath the light covering of his shirt and curl into the masculine growth of hair on his chest.

As his flesh tautened she wondered if her shameless fingers had given her away. Did he feel their quivering urge to touch, know the frightening depth of emotion he was arousing in her? She looked up in anxiety and her hope that he might not have perceived anything different in her died when she saw the dawning cynicism in his eyes.

"Wanting to find something else out?"

"I don't know what you mean."

Shuddering in shame and rebellion she used her hands as a lever to push herself away from him, at the same time shaking off his hands. She knew that he let her do this, that if he'd exerted himself to stop her she would have been powerless to escape. As her hands dropped loosely to her sides his crept round her waist, pushing upward under her sweater, following her spine. She felt the tingling in her breasts as he unfastened the clasp of her bra. She tried to swallow, but her throat wouldn't constrict, as if she'd lost command of the muscles. Her breathing was similarly defective and the blood seemed to be pumping through her body at twice its normal speed.

Her heart throbbed fiercely as his hands moved round to the front. The tingling lightness of his touch scalded and sensitized her flesh. His thumbs rubbed sensuous circles round her nipples, then withdrew. As before, his lips moved down to take their place, lightly and moistly taking her left nipple between them, biting gently, as if on some precious fruit, then pausing.

She waited, her breath held and his name hovering on her lips. She dared not speak, but she had no clear idea whether she was afraid that he wouldn't stop if he knew how he was affecting her—or that he would.

His breath was hot on her throbbing breast; surely he could feel her heart beating against the warm flesh of his mouth. Then his tongue slipped back onto the pebble-hard tip of her breast and she shuddered against him as he resumed the maddening caresses of a moment before. His fingers teased gently at her other nipple, which tautened further in response, flames darting along her skin.

His other hand slipped to her back and then down along her spine and beneath her jeans, moving with tormenting slowness over the firm, rounded curves of her buttocks. Teasingly, always teasingly, his mouth and hands sent her quivering along the path of mindless sensation, her breath coming in long gasps of agonized delight.

And then, suddenly, he stopped. His hands returned to his sides and he lifted his head. The cool air of the house chilled the overheated, moistened flesh of her breast, and the desire that had been coiling and uncoiling within her, leaving a hollow feeling beneath the pit of her stomach, subsided as shame coursed through her.

Only then did she realize he was playing that macabre teasing game again. Demonstrating, with even greater boldness, the power he could wield over her, the command he had over himself. Proving, in case she hadn't got the message the first time, that he was capable of driving her to dizzy heights of desire while remaining immune himself.

"There. I'm sure you can manage the rest yourself —getting out of those damp things and into something dry."

She slid her hand over the seat of her jeans in a gesture of restraint. How she would have loved to slap that smirk off his face.

"Thank you," she said stiffly. She could have been

saying thank you for anything. Thank you, I can manage. Thank you for bringing the towels. Thank you for humiliating me as I have never been humiliated before. Or—and this one was somewhat belated—Thank you for braving the loch and coming to get me.

"I wondered when you'd get round to that."

"Don't make it sound as though I'm ill-mannered. You haven't given me much time to say anything. I'm exceedingly grateful. I might have survived on my own, but I have no guarantee of that. It was a lucky chance that you missed me and came after me."

He said very slowly, injecting his words with a specific importance, "You can thank Angus that I did."

"Angus? He's . . . here?"

"At this moment he's thawing out in the kitchen. I came looking for you when he arrived. If Angus hadn't come I wouldn't have realized you weren't in the house."

"He brought the boat out in this? He wouldn't have attempted it in this unless . . . Oh, no! Ian . . . ?"

He nodded.

"Is he . . . ?" She didn't seem capable of finishing a sentence. Not that it mattered. Her meaning was clear.

"No. But there's no knowing how much longer he can hold on. His mind is wandering. No one can be certain how much he's aware of. But he's asking for you."

"For me? But I can't . . ."

"Oh, yes, you can. I'm taking you to his bedside and you are going to play the part of loving fiancée. If you don't, it will be the last thing you'll ever be asked to do because I personally will break your neck. Take off those damp things, give yourself a brisk rub down, put some dry clothes on and then we can get the hell off this benighted island."

"It seems I have no alternative."

"You do. The alternative is for me to take them off for you."

"Get out. Out, do you hear? I'll be as quick as I can, damn you!"

It was a nightmare journey through the icy, mist-wreathed waters and only Angus's skill kept the boat on course and got them safely to the mainland, where Maxwell's car was waiting for them. Maxwell took over and drove the car to the hospital. Snowplows had been out in force and made a good job of opening the major roads, with a backup of sand trucks to keep them that way. Even though Maxwell tempered his desire for speed to meet the conditions it was still a hazardous journey. Gemma, whose nerves were strung on steel pegs, heaved a sigh of relief as he signaled and turned to drive through the dreaded hospital gates. The real ordeal—being presented to Ian as his fiancée—was still before her.

Poor Ian. Her heart bled for him. How could she do this to him? How could she get out of it? She had tried and tried and tried, but no way could she convince Maxwell that she wasn't Glenda. It was stupid and frustrating and it was going to cause un-necessary suffering, and Ian had suffered enough already.

They were shown into a waiting room by a Scottish nurse who said she would alert Sister of their arrival. It was comfortable by hospital standards, more like a sitting room with its deep armchairs, restful green walls and newspapers and magazines scattered on various surfaces. This room was made available to people who were visiting a sick relative or a close friend. Could anyone lose himself in daily events or escapist reading while burdened with the sort of worry entailed? She didn't think she would have the concentration. It was an idle conjecture, meant to take her mind off having to face Ian.

She absentmindedly pushed at a newspaper—and then grabbed it up and began to read the headlines with avid interest.

GLENDA CHANNING, HEIRESS TO THE CHANNING EMPIRE, STILL MISSING. FRANTIC FATHER UPS REWARD. In small print it went on to say that Mr. Clifford Channing, the missing girl's father, admitted to the possibility that his daughter might have gone into hiding on her own. If this was the case he appealed most strongly to her to return home, or at least to contact him.

Maxwell came up behind her, curious to see what had captured her attention, and read the headlines over her shoulder.

She twisted her neck round to look at him, but the entreaty in her eyes was lost on him.

"Do you still insist that you aren't Glenda Channing?" he said curtly.

There wasn't a photograph of Glenda, not even of the usual smudgy, barely recognizable newspaper sort, but there was a description. Blue eyes, blonde hair, petite build, age twenty-two. Gemma was puzzled. What did this mean? Glenda certainly hadn't been kidnapped. It was obvious that she had gone into hiding somewhere on her own. Why would she want to disappear like that? Gemma had always felt that there was something, a key factor, which she didn't know. She'd think about it later and try to figure something out when her mind was clearer.

"My eyes are gray," she informed Maxwell, pointing out the one discrepancy in the description.

"So they are," he said scathingly. "So what? Obviously a misprint."

"What will it take to convince you?" she said, sounding both despairing and haughty. "For Ian to denounce me? Or his distress at having a strange girl masquerading as his fiancée?"

He didn't even gratify that with a reply, although he awarded her a long and searching look. His mouth fixed into a straight, obdurate line. He hunched his shoulders, a bitter gesture that seemed to imply that he was steeling himself against her, and walked away.

A grave-faced doctor arrived with the ward sister at his heels. The doctor said something to Maxwell, Maxwell replied, and then the heads turned in her direction. Partly by assumption and partly by lip-reading Gemma gathered that her relationship had to be explained before she would be allowed near Ian's bed. The looks the doctor and the ward sister gave her were cutting, and she didn't blame them. If she really had been Ian's fiancée, and if she hadn't bothered to visit him before now, their disapproval and contempt would have been justified. She dipped her head, feeling as wretched as if she really had deserted Ian in his need.

Ian was in a private ward. Two women sat by his bed, one small, motherly, and dumpy with a round face and a brave smile forcing itself through her grief; the other woman was much younger. She had a broad face tapering into a narrow chin, set upon a swan-like neck. Her coloring was striking, red hair with green eyes. She had long elegant hands and feet to complement her height and she was the most beautiful woman that Gemma had ever seen. But it was a cold beauty, with no stirring of warmth beneath the hard perfection of her porcelain features.

She turned her head and there was no welcome in the look she gave Gemma; that was saved for Maxwell. She leaped to her feet with the grace of a dancer and threw herself into his arms. "Thank God you got here. I thought you weren't going to make it in time."

"Bless you, Fiona," he said. For all his great height he didn't have to bend very far to drop a kiss on her forehead. "Say a quick hello to Glenda," he instructed. "Glenda—Fiona."

They shook hands and Gemma's heart sank, not because of the unfriendly lightness of the other girl's handshake, which almost amounted to distaste, but because Fiona and Glenda hadn't met before. She realized that she had been clinging to the hope that Glenda and Fiona had met previously and that Fiona would say, "But this isn't Glenda."

There was still the other woman, but that expectation was just as quickly dashed.

"Glenda—Morag," Maxwell introduced tersely.

The crinkling of the eyes in the round, apple face was the first intimation of welcome, even though the voice was tart. "Come away in with you." She got to her feet. "Take my chair." Her tone stilled any demur Gemma might have made. "It's been fit to break a body's heart, the poor wee laddie calling for you and you not here." Her voice softened and filled with love as she turned to the figure on the bed. "She's here, Master Ian, so fret nae mair, bonnie laddie."

Even so, Gemma still needed the push Maxwell gave her to go forward.

A voice, so weak as to be barely audible, said, "Is that really you, Glenda?"

A hand groped on the coverlet. Her own closed round it, gently, so as not to hurt. What else could she do? It was obvious that Ian was so full of pain-killing drugs that he was past recognizing anyone. She had no compunction in telling the lie.

"Yes, it's Glenda. I'm here, darling."

A deep sigh of content came from his lips. His eyes

were almost closed, as if he was very weary and
wanted nothing more than to sleep for a long, long
time.

Gemma had no idea how long she sat there,
holding Ian's hand. Her own arm went dead with
holding it too long in one position. She would have
liked to have changed hands, but Ian looked so
tranquil that she didn't have the heart to disturb him
and so she endured the pain and discomfort.

It was Maxwell who finally extricated her fingers
from Ian's. She rubbed the numbed tips, trying to get
the circulation back, and it wasn't until he took her by
the elbows to assist her out of her chair that she
understood.

"Is he . . . ?"

"Yes, it's all over. We must go now. We're in the
way here."

"Yes. Yes, of course."

Tears filled her eyes, as they would have done for
any young life cut off so abruptly. It was tragic, such a
waste.

Maxwell said somberly, "He would never have
walked again. For Ian that would have been worse
than death. I've heard others say that time and time
again and I've always thought it sounded so heartless.
You've got to go through it yourself to understand. But
it really was for the best. I'm glad we got here in time."

"Yes. So am I."

To quote Maxwell's words, it was all over. Maxwell
had done what he'd set out to do, bring her to Ian's
bedside, although he had hoped it would be to aid his
brother's recovery and not to say goodbye. There was
nothing to keep her here now. Much as she wanted
her release, she felt sad at heart. She hadn't wanted it
this way.

Fiona and Morag had gone on ahead and were

talking to Angus in the waiting room. Gemma's feet dragged. Every step was taking her one step farther away from Maxwell.

Resentment whipped through her at the cruel twist of fate that had brought her and Maxwell together in circumstances where there could be no future for them.

"Ian's at rest," she heard Maxwell say. "It's the living who matter now."

She was still busily pursuing her own thoughts. If only there was something she could do, some way to stay on and fight for Maxwell's love, but there wasn't.

Defeated she said, "It only remains for me to go home now."

"That's where you're wrong." His eyes were dark with suffering, but he was as indomitable as ever. "It only remains for us to get married."

9

~œœœœœœœœœ~

At the time it didn't seem in any way like a strange proposal; only the circumstances leading up to it were strange and it never occurred to her not to take it seriously. All she could concentrate on was that Maxwell wasn't going to let her go and that he wanted to marry her. She could hardly expect him to go into raptures and declare his love in these clinical hospital surroundings. With Ian's death weighing heavily on his mind it wouldn't be right.

He was still under the impression that she was Glenda Channing, of course, but he had proposed to a girl, not a name, and that could be sorted out later. For now she slid her hand into his and the act of giving it to him was her answer as she walked by his side with a much lighter step.

It was a sad and for the most part silent journey to Glenross and the house where for generations the Ross family had lived. As before, Maxwell drove.

Gemma sat by his side; Fiona, Morag, and Angus occupied the back of the car. Morag sniffed into her handkerchief and Angus made murmurs of comfort. But no one really spoke until Maxwell turned off the main road and brought the car to a stop before the tall ornate gates giving access to a long, tree-lined drive, and even then he was the one to break the silence.

"We're home," he said for Gemma's benefit.

Angus was already getting out of the car to open the gates. Home? thought Gemma as Maxwell drove through, stopping the car to wait until Angus had closed the gates and resumed his seat.

The word "home" conjured up a picture of warmth and love and contentment of the heart. A place where you shut the door on the cares of the world. A cozy refuge. When it came into view she could have hugged herself for joy. Solid and square, large enough to be comfortable but not too large to be without a soul. It was just the kind of house she had always dreamed of coming home to. Some trick of the moonlight—the particular way the light slanted onto the latticed windows—touched her dreamer's fancy and gave the house an inner glow that Gemma took as a good omen.

She could hardly believe it when the car drove straight by. She must have gasped, she might even have said something, or perhaps, with uncanny Scots instinct, Fiona read her thoughts.

A dry laugh came from behind, mocking her stupidity. "That's the lodge."

"You'll see the house when we get round this next bend," Maxwell said, and his voice seemed to contain some of Fiona's amusement.

It gave Gemma an outsider's feeling of being ganged up on by two people who were very close.

That thought was lost as the soaring gray-stoned house loomed in front of her astonished eyes. Huge, austere, perhaps it did have a certain commanding beauty, but she was too overawed to see it. Steps led up to a door of fortress-like proportions, and to Gemma's eyes it looked every bit as forbidding. Even the kindly benevolence of the moonlight couldn't lessen this effect or still her qualms. A sick, cold feeling of apprehension walked with her and she lagged noticeably behind the others as she entered that imposing door.

The inside, still a long way from homey by Gemma's concept of the word, was such a vast improvement over the exterior that she felt the first easing of relief in her throat.

Despite the lateness of the hour a young maid, who answered to the name of Jeanie, had waited up and Morag sent her to prepare a room for Gemma. The housekeeper then set about preparing a meal and the thought of food made Gemma feel better still. She realized with some surprise that the last meal she and Maxwell had eaten was breakfast. No wonder she was almost passing out.

As a matter of course Morag arranged three settings at the dining table, then, on Maxwell's instructions, added two more places for herself and Angus. Gemma was glad that he had relaxed the formalities to invite his housekeeper and her husband to share his table. She wished he'd taken it a step further, as she would have preferred the informality of the kitchen.

Morag brought in a huge ham and a joint of beef, which she carved at the side table, transferring generous portions to the plates.

Maxwell stated baldly, making no effort to lead up to his words, "Glenda and I are going to be married."

He had to tell them sometime, but not like that. It was too soon, and the words were too matter-of-fact, like a business arrangement, and because the table was between them he couldn't take hold of Gemma's hand. The announcement should have been made later, much later, when she'd had time to get acquainted with both Fiona and Morag, because although Morag was an employee she seemed so much a part of the family. And it should have been done with Maxwell's arm sliding round her as he pulled her to his side, the grief he felt at the loss of his brother softened under a glow of pride, perhaps giving a self-conscious laugh as he said, "Gemma—" by then she would have convinced him of her real identity, of course— "Gemma and I are very much in love and we are going to be married."

This way wasn't fair to her, and it wasn't fair to Fiona and Morag and Angus, either. Particularly to Fiona, who looked as if the bottom had suddenly fallen out of her world.

Gemma cast her eyes down and pretended to be absorbed in the plate of cold meat before her, but all she could see were the uneasy glances that passed between Morag and Angus and Fiona's stricken disbelief. Although Morag's and Angus's approval mattered, because she was family, Fiona's reaction was the one that counted most and Gemma knew she would be haunted by the look she had seen on Fiona's face for a long time. Not only had Maxwell done it all wrong, but he'd got his facts wrong, too. Fiona hadn't been interested in Ian in the way that Maxwell thought. It was too early for Gemma to tell whether or not Fiona loved Maxwell, but one thing was absolutely certain in her mind: Fiona's sights had been set on being his bride.

As soon as the meal was over she was dismissed and sent to her room so that the remaining foursome could talk. At least, it seemed that way to Gemma.

"You must be tired, Glenda. Jeanie will show you to your room," Maxwell said, and it had the peremptory ring of a command.

Perhaps it was silly of her, selfish even, to want to drag Maxwell away from the others when he'd only just got back, but she had hoped that he would come with her. She had anticipated a good-night kiss and a kind word to say that everything was going to be all right, because people in love sense things and he would know about her fears. Then she wouldn't feel so lost and frightened. But he hadn't mentioned the word love. Yet why else would he want to marry her? If it was only physical he would have thought in terms of an affair. He wouldn't have proposed something as long-standing as marriage. But he should have said that he loved her. That wasn't something a girl could take for granted.

Jeanie took her up to her room. It was spacious, despite the large and cumbersome, by current standards, bedroom suite, which was handmade and had that satin patina you only find on old and cared-for furniture. It was a much grander room than the one she had occupied at Iola, but it didn't make her feel as welcome.

All the way up the stairs Jeanie had been casting curious glances at her. Now she said, "Will you be wanting anything, ma'am?"

Gemma replied that she wouldn't.

Jeanie said, "I'll be away to my bed, then. Good night."

"Good night, Jeanie. And thank you."

She wanted something. But it wasn't anything that

Jeanie could give her. She took off her own lavender wool dress, glad that she had put that on and not something of Fiona's which Maxwell had dug out for her to wear while on Iola. Fiona resented her being here. It would have made the situation more intolerable still if she'd been wearing the other girl's clothes. It would be bad enough having to confess to Fiona that she had borrowed some of her things.

As she got into bed her feet touched a hot water bottle. It was the only bit of warmth she had felt in this house. No matter whose idea it was—had Jeanie acted on her own initiative or upon Morag's instructions?—she was grateful for the comforting thought.

With so much on her mind she thought she would have difficulty in dropping off, but not only did she sleep the sleep of the exhausted, she overslept.

It was half-past nine when she very apologetically presented herself to Morag, who was in the kitchen, up to her wrists in flour.

"I'm sorry. I had no idea of the time."

"I had a peep at you earlier to ask if you wanted a tea tray, but you were dead to the world, so I let you be. I'll get you some breakfast," Morag said, taking her hands out of the baking bowl and going over to wash them at the kitchen sink.

"Please don't trouble. I'm not really hungry."

Morag clicked her tongue and rebuked her. "It's important for you to have regular nourishment and breakfast is one meal that should never be skipped."

"I don't understand everyone's preoccupation with feeding me," Gemma said grumblingly, because Maxwell had been equally insistent on her having regular meals.

Morag made no comment but sent Gemma a slightly cold look as she took bacon from the fridge and an egg from its holder and then went to the stove to give the porridge a stir.

"You don't approve of Mr. Ross marrying me, do you, Morag?" Gemma asked, taking her place at the kitchen table before Morag had any ideas of shunting her into the dining room.

"It's not my place to approve or disapprove of anything the master does," Morag replied pedantically. "I can see . . ." She stopped.

"Go on."

". . . that he would look upon it as his duty," Morag said with a shrug. "The only decent way out."

"I don't understand what you mean. You know that Mr. Ross, well, that he took me to Iola by force?"

"Aye. My Angus being a party to it, I had to know that. I didn't hold with such carryings on and I told him so. Yet, in Master Ian's interest, what else could he do? Even if it wasn't a praiseworthy thing he did, his purpose was above reproach."

His purpose had been to take Gemma—or rather, Glenda—to Ian's bedside. That accomplished, why did Morag think that Maxwell would look upon it as his duty to marry her, that he would consider it the only decent solution?

"I know we were alone on the island." In these times it seemed preposterous to have to explain this. "But we didn't go to bed together, you know."

"I should think not!" Morag said, and she couldn't have looked more shocked if Gemma had instead confessed to days and nights of unremitting passion.

If Morag didn't think they'd slept together, although sleeping together wasn't a reason for getting married these days, what did she mean? Chewing on her lip, Gemma said, "Where is Mr. Ross now?"

"Out on estate business. A place this size doesn't run itself. Although my Angus is his right-hand man and has full authority in the master's absence, there's still a pile-up of things that need his personal attention."

"Is the estate very large, Morag?"

"Aye, by any standards. There's a section reserved for timber, and then the master holds the rights to some of the finest salmon fishing in Scotland. But it's the home farm that takes up most of his time. A small part of the estate is divided into individual farms which are let to tenant farmers. He takes his duties as a landlord very seriously. No matter how hard pressed he is, it's never at the neglect of others."

"You have a very high respect for him, haven't you, Morag?"

"Aye, and so will you have if—" She clamped her mouth shut, holding her runaway tongue.

"If I'm around long enough to know him that well?" queried Gemma, lifting the implication out of the air.

"I didn't say that."

"You implied it. Mr. Ross and I *are* going to be married. Don't you think the wedding will take place?" She knew it wouldn't if Fiona had anything to do with it. "Is that it, Morag?"

"It'll take place, well enough."

"Then what? Don't you think it will last?"

With a regretful shake of her head, Morag said, "I don't hold with divorce any more than I hold with a lot of other things which are regarded as standard procedure these days."

"Divorce?" Now Gemma was the one to be shocked. "Who's talking about divorce?"

"No one. You're flummoxing me, making me say things I shouldn't. I'd be obliged if you'd eat your breakfast, Miss, and let me get on with my work."

Upon which Morag set a bowl of porridge in front of her and presented her with her back, and no amount of probing could get another word out of her, on that subject, at least.

Gemma knew that she must get word of her whereabouts to Miss Davies and Barry as soon as possible, and with this in mind she decided to search the house for a telephone. She thought about spilling out the whole story to Morag and enlisting her help in getting in touch with people who might be worrying about her, but realized that it wasn't fair to involve Morag. A person can only serve one master and she wouldn't like to think she was responsible for getting Morag to do something she might consider underhanded.

She discovered a telephone in the drawing room. She didn't want either Fiona or Morag to overhear her, so she wondered if there was another one somewhere more private. She found what she was looking for in a book-lined study. The phone was on the desk and she judged by the number of file cabinets around that this was the room where Maxwell attended to the paperwork involved in running the estate.

Although it would be easier to phone while Maxwell was out she didn't care if he came back and caught her. She wouldn't be saying anything that she hadn't already said to him many times.

She would have preferred to speak to Miss Davies, her superior at work, but after pondering on this for a moment she dialed Barry's office number. She was conscious that she was making a long-distance call without first obtaining Maxwell's permission. Miss Davies didn't always grasp the point very quickly. It would be less expensive, and more practical, to contact Barry and ask him to pass the message on. Also, there was another consideration. She wondered if she might ask Barry to come up to Scotland to help convince Maxwell that she wasn't Glenda, something she couldn't possibly suggest to Miss Davies at her age and with the roads as they were. She was quite relieved to find that the telephone was working, having half expected the lines to be down.

She announced her name to Barry's secretary and a few moments later heard his voice inquiring urgently, "Gemma, is that you? What's going on?"

"Barry, it's a long and very involved story. I've no right to ask this of you, but I'm desperate. Please don't let me down. The fact is, I need you. Will you come—"

"What the hell are you playing at?"

The words came from behind. Maxwell's tone was bitter and there was black murder in his eyes as he wrenched the phone from her hand and crashed it down on its cradle.

"Why did you do that?" she protested. "Why didn't you listen? You might have learned something."

"I did. I learned what a little tramp you are."

Hot color ran up her neck. She realized she was trembling as much from fear at what he intended to do next as from choking humiliation and anger. He hadn't bothered to close the door when he came in and it was open for anyone to hear.

"You are never to speak to him again," he commanded autocratically.

"Sometimes I think you must be off your rocker," she said, trying to scrape past him, not sure whether she meant to close the door for privacy or run from him in cowardice until he'd simmered down.

The choice wasn't hers to make. He caught hold of her wrists and brought her forcibly up against his chest.

"There are times when I think I am. Instead of forbidding you to have any further contact with your boyfriend perhaps I'd show more sense if I packed you off to him. How dare you tell him that you're in desperate need of him? Begging him to come to you like . . . like I don't know what."

"It wasn't like that, and if you were reasoning properly you'd know it wasn't."

"No?" he sneered.

"I refuse to talk to you while you're in this mood, so please let me pass."

"I'll talk to you in any mood I like. And you're going nowhere."

"I hate you," she said through clenched teeth.

"There are times when you're not my favorite person, either, but it seems that we're stuck with one another."

He glared down at her and she found herself unable to look away.

In one movement her wrists were released and she was pushed from him. He walked toward the door and she heaved a sigh of relief which was smartly swallowed as, instead of continuing through the door as she had hoped, he slammed it viciously shut and then twisted the key in the lock.

Backing away from the insane, dark torment in his eyes she stammered nervously, "Wh-what are you going to do?"

"Give you something to hate me for. I'll get the truth if I have to beat it out of you."

"I've never lied to you," she insisted, knowing in every nerve in her body that even as he threatened to lift his hand to her in violence he wanted to kiss her, swamp her mouth with his, slide his hands down her back and line her body to his.

And then, his anger still there, as unquenchable as

the passion that was burning him up, driving him on, he was doing just that, tilting her chin and forcing her back to arch to such an extent that she had to grab hold of his shirt front to prevent herself from falling over. And then his hands were moving with inexorable precision down her spine, splaying out to compel her body even more intimately close. She felt his desire; the heat of his hunger for her seeped through her clothes and found a reciprocal flame.

She closed her eyes in bitter desperation and wished for an immunity that did not come as the combined forces of his anger and his need of her searched for appeasement. His mouth savaged hers; his hands were ungentle as they found their way beneath the material of her dress to travel across her shoulder blades, encircle her throat and explore the vulnerable hollows along her collarbone. A pulse quivered in her throat in recognition of her helplessness and fragility. One hand dropped to her breast in a light touch that was almost an act of reverence. The contrast was sweet, oh, so sweet. Following the instincts that were teasing her she wriggled open the buttons on his shirt, finding a way inside and letting her fingers delight in the hard strength of his muscular chest and wind into the masculine growth of hair she had known instinctively would be there. Simultaneously his fingers delighted her breasts, fondling each in turn with tender care through the thin layers of material. The pulse in her throat throbbed more wildly with the gently increased pressure of his caresses; her mouth was subjected to kisses that drained her resistance to the dregs. She clung weakly to him in a gesture that conveyed submission, total and unconditional, and rampant invitation.

He responded to the invitation with a passion that

was shattering in its intensity. She was wearing the lavender dress again and his right hand left her breast and dropped to her hemline. His fingers teased gently at the material before slipping underneath it to slide softly up her leg. He drew light patterns on her thigh, those tormentingly knowing fingers sliding ever higher up the slick fabric of her nylons, leaving traces of fire on the sensitized skin beneath.

At last, after heart-stopping moments in which she felt an anticipation so great that she could hardly keep herself from taking his hand and forcing it those last few inches, his finger flicked gently at the heart of her desire. She shuddered, gasped, then bit her lip in an agony of wanting. Never had she known a need so great. Then his whole strong palm closed on her, cupping the mound of her desire and sliding slowly back and forth. Her knees turned to water and she trembled against him, her breath rasping in her throat as he forced her ever closer to release.

A loud banging on the door brought them to their senses. A voice called out, "Are you all right in there?" And then, after a moment, "Mr. Ross, will ye not answer?"

"It's all right, Morag. Go about your business." To Gemma he said, "After the commotion, the calm is sometimes more worrying. Poor Morag probably thought that I'd murdered you." His voice was gruff, as if he was wondering how his anger had channeled into this, but he seemed totally unaffected by the passion that still held Gemma shuddering in its grasp.

She did her dress up and attempted to smooth her hair into some kind of order. Without saying another word, his icy composure once again intact, Maxwell turned on his heel, unlocked the door and walked out of the room.

She had no option but to follow his example. She couldn't stay there forever, although she would have liked to. Goodness only knew what Morag must think, but she had to be faced sometime.

But it was Fiona's contempt she ran into first. Trust Fiona to hear everything and then complete her humiliation by staying to crow.

"Well?" she said, squaring her chin to the older girl.

Fiona's laugh was dry and brittle. "I'm sorry if I'm staring. We're simply not used to slanging matches like that. Poor Maxwell, I feel so sorry for him."

Gemma resolved not to let Fiona draw her. All the same, she couldn't have been thinking straight because it was absurdly ill-timed to say, "I borrowed some of your things to wear at Iola. I hope you don't mind too much."

"Some things I don't mind your borrowing, and my clothes fit that category." The implication was, my clothes but not my man. "They must have looked ludicrous on you. You hardly match up to me . . . in height," she said, so belatedly that she might as well have left that addition off.

"I don't match up to you, period," Gemma replied.

Fiona's eyes narrowed and glinted dangerously. "But it's you whom Maxwell is marrying. Why don't you say it?" she taunted.

"I don't have to. You've just said it for me."

"Don't sound so damned triumphant! How can he be such a fool? There's no guarantee that the brat you're carrying is Ian's."

"Would you mind repeating that?" Gemma said weakly.

Fiona didn't have to repeat it. That was it, of course, the missing piece of the puzzle. Glenda was carrying a child. Ian's child? That's why Maxwell had asked her to marry him, not because he loved her, but to give the baby the Ross name. He only wanted to marry her to get control of the baby. No one expected the marriage to last. That's what Morag had meant when they had spoken on the subject earlier.

"You didn't honestly think that Maxwell had asked you to marry him because he felt anything for you?" Fiona asked, tossing her head back and laughing shrilly.

"That's enough, Miss Fiona," Morag's voice cut in, startling Gemma, who hadn't realized she was there. It was obvious, though, that she had been listening. "It's wicked of you to make such an accusation. Of course it's Master Ian's bairn."

"Shut up, Morag, and remember your place," Fiona said, redirecting her venom. "You've been shown too much leniency in this house. It's time you remembered that you're only a servant."

Morag's head went down. She muttered something under her breath that Gemma didn't catch and shuffled off to the kitchen.

Fiona sent Gemma a last killing look and flounced off in the opposite direction.

Gemma didn't have to think about which one of them to follow, Morag, obviously. She had to get the answers from someone and Morag's account would be fair and not barbed.

Morag was slumped over the table, a handkerchief to her nose. Gemma lightly touched her shoulder to let her know that she was there and pulled out a companion chair for herself.

"I'm sorry, Morag. I feel responsible. Fiona was angry with me. I'm sure she didn't mean what she said to you."

"T'wasn't your fault. She meant it, all right. That's

been brewing for some time. If ever Miss Fiona becomes mistress here I'll pack my bags and be out the door like a shot out of a gun."

"Morag, what you said about . . . about a baby."

"These things happen," Morag admitted on a sniff. "I'm not condemning you for that."

"So what are you condemning me for?"

"Need you ask?" Morag questioned in shocked indignation. "Abortion—that's a word we never heard used in my day, praise be—is against the preaching of our good Lord. How you could even consider such a thing is beyond my ken! Of course, I know it's what your father wanted," she said, wringing her hands in distress. "And with Master Ian, God rest his soul, not able to stand by your side, I can see how easy it must have been for you to fall under your father's influence. But that's no excuse for the sin you intended. Mr. Ross had to do something to prevent such a wicked deed, a transgression against everything that's decent and honorable. The blood in me boils just to think about it."

A strangled gasp came from Gemma's lips. "So . . . Maxwell abducted me and took me to Iola, a place so remote that I'd no chance of escaping from it, not to be there when, if, Ian came round, but . . . until it was too late to have the abortion? Is that what you're saying, Morag?"

"Aye, lassie. This bairn is sorely wanted. It will ease a lot of pain."

"Oh . . . Morag," she despaired, shaking her head to rid it of the confusion this new turn-up had wrought, trying to *think*. "Where is Maxwell? Did you see where he went when he came out of his study?"

"Up the stairs to his room, I should imagine. But there's no telling whether he's still there now."

* * *

But he was. He opened the door to her impatient knock, positioning himself to bar her entry into the room. "Well? What do you want?" he demanded.

"To come in, please," she said, shivering, but not letting his icy countenance put her off. Nothing must put her off. This time she must convince him.

Grudgingly he stood aside. She walked past him, into the room, and waited until he'd closed the door.

"Thank you, Maxwell." She didn't know how to start and she just blurted out what she had been saying all along. "I'm not Glenda."

"Oh, no!"

She sighed. "Will you please admit the possibility that I might be telling the truth? We need a starting point to talk from. It's vital that we talk this out."

"I'll go along with that," he said harshly. "Talk."

Not very confidence inspiring, but better than nothing, if only just. "Fiona let something slip which I knew nothing about and Morag confirmed it. I didn't know that Glenda was pregnant."

For a moment she thought he was going to laugh in her face, and it wouldn't have been pleasant laughter, that was for sure. But then he said, "All right. We'll play it your way. We'll pretend that you aren't Glenda and that this is all new to you."

"I am not Glenda; it *is* all new to me. *Please,* cut the mockery and explain the facts."

His eyes narrowed, but he did just that. "Even before he knew about the baby, Ian wanted to marry—" fractional pause—"*Glenda,*" he said with a meaningful emphasis she could have done without. "He was over the moon when she told him. As far as he was concerned, it just brought the wedding date forward."

"But Glenda wasn't so thrilled, I take it?"

"It would be fairer to say that Clifford Channing wasn't pleased. He didn't want Ian for a son-in-law and suggested a way out of her . . . er . . . difficulties. Ian was going to see him, to try to reason with him, when he crashed his car. And even you, no matter who you insist you are, know the outcome of that."

"I'm sorry, Maxwell, truly sorry for bringing the pain of your brother's death back. With Ian in hospital, Glenda would have felt lost. It would have been natural for her to turn to her father. So the abortion was his idea—yes?"

"Yes. He'd even got as far as booking her into a very expensive clinic. I received a panic letter from . . . from *her*," he said with great difficulty, as if he thought he should be saying from *you*. "Although we'd never met, as Ian's brother she felt that I was the obvious person to approach for help. She didn't want to be pressured into doing something she could later regret. I got her on the phone straight away and told her that abortion was out of the question. I said I would take her away—to a place where she would be free of her father's authority and the bad influence he was having on her, somewhere he would never find her. Although she agreed, and even suggested a point where it would be convenient for me to pick her up, I sensed a certain reluctance."

"I should think so!" Gemma said, flying to Glenda's defense. "What sort of escape would that be? She'd just be swapping one dominant power for another." One bully for another, she might just as well have said.

"That's ridiculous! I was out to help her."

"In his own way, so was her father, even though what he wanted her to do was wrong. And so," she said, changing to a meditative tone, "I came along driving Glenda's car and you quite naturally thought I was Glenda and that I was keeping the appointment."

"When you started to object I assumed you'd changed your mind about coming with me. It was something I'd half expected anyway. You were carrying my brother's child, and no way was I going to let you get rid of it. With or without your permission, I was taking you somewhere beyond your father's reach. I'd already set the wheels in motion to take you to Iola. Angus had that side of the operation in hand—opening up the house and laying in provisions. I saw no reason for a change of plan where that was concerned, because I reckoned it would be the last place your father would look for you. I intended to keep you there until it was medically impossible for you to have an abortion."

With a dull little ache she realized that he had gone back to thinking of her as Glenda. "It must be as you assumed. Glenda apparently did change her mind. She was acting very strangely when we met up in the cafe. I remember that she said it should be her decision. She was most insistent about that. I didn't know what she was talking about at the time, but now it all fits in. Glenda must have known that you wouldn't let her change her mind about going into hiding, so she fobbed me off on you in her place. It could have been a spur-of-the-moment decision, arrived at when she passed me on the road into Ashford that morning. She'd have known it was my day off because it was later than my normal time for going to work. She'd also have known my habits, that I normally park in the square on shopping days, and in a town of that size it wouldn't have been difficult to find me. She made up that phony story about having to take her car in for a minor repair job, conned me into letting her use my car and then got me to drive her car back, knowing that I'd have to pass the spot where she'd arranged to meet you to get home. The switch of handbags was something she couldn't have counted on, but it was a stroke of genius, because that convinced you that I was Glenda Channing. Nothing I said could make you think otherwise."

"Rather elaborate lengths to go to. If, just *if*, it was as you say, wouldn't it have been easier for her just not to turn up?"

"Would you have let it rest at that?"

"No, I wouldn't. I would have hunted you down."

"There's your answer. That's why she did what she did. She planted me in her place to get you off her back and then she went off somewhere on her own to think things out."

"No more play-acting, Glenda. It was a good try and I award you full marks for ingenuity, but you're not getting away with it, or away from me. You'll never escape me. The child you're carrying will have its rightful name. I made that vow to myself as I stood by Ian's bed."

"Ian . . . of course!" Ian's acceptance of her would have clinched it with him. "I know what you're thinking. At the hospital . . . what else could I do? Ian *didn't* recognize me; he was too heavily sedated for that. I faked it; I pretended to be Glenda. In my place anyone would have done the same, wanted to give him some peace in his last moments. But I did it for you as much as for Ian. You dragged me to his bedside. I knew it would have caused you untold distress to have presented the wrong girl. But I can't fake a baby, not even for you."

"If you're saying that you'd already done the deed

before I picked you up, I don't believe you." There was menace in his eyes, black cynicism in the smile on his lips. "You wouldn't have had time."

"I'm saying it isn't possible. To have a baby you've got to . . . got to have . . . Don't you understand?" she screamed at him. "It just isn't possible."

10

She would have run from the room but he anticipated this and grabbed her by the wrists, looking deep
into her storm-gray, tear-flecked eyes. It was going
round and round in her mind. He doesn't want to
marry you to keep you by his side. He doesn't love
you. Doesn't love you . . . doesn't love you.

He had only asked her to marry him to give his
brother's child its rightful name, a child she wasn't
even carrying. For one wild moment she wished that
she was, wished she was Glenda and with child,
because then he would marry her. She wriggled her
fingers free of his and drew them nervously across her
taut, flat stomach. Time, ally or enemy, and she wasn't
sure which, would prove her right, and then he
wouldn't need to have anything more to do with her
and he would send her away.

It altered nothing. She didn't want to go, but even if

it resulted in her being sent away this very moment she still had to convince him. With a surge of desperation she took up the issue again.

"You must believe me, Maxwell, and believing me you must do something while there's still time, *if* there's still time to prevent a tragedy. It's obvious that Glenda has gone off somewhere on her own to make the decision herself. Her disappearance was reported to the press by her father, who's offering a reward, so he doesn't know where she is. When she planted me in her place it must have been in her mind to get away from you both, you and her father. All she wanted to do was make up her own mind, something neither of you would let her do. The decision could go either way. You must prepare yourself for the possibility that when you do find her . . . it might be too late."

"Could you take a lie to these lengths?" His black-olive eyes raked her face. "Is it possible that you might be telling the truth? If you aren't Glenda, why did you consent to marry me?"

"I . . . don't understand."

"Don't be obtuse. You must have had a reason for saying yes." He caught hold of her wrists again, shaking them as though to force the answer from her. "If it wasn't to give your unborn child its rightful name, what reason did you have?"

Reluctant to say, unwilling to reveal her heart and admit that for some time now she had been in love with him, she fell back on evasion. "As I remember it, I didn't say yes or no. You told me we were going to be married. As far as you were concerned that settled the matter."

"Ah . . . yes. That I cannot deny."

"I won't hold you to it. You only proposed to me to give your brother's child a name. There isn't going to be a child, at least . . . I'm not carrying it. So you can't still want to marry me. Can you?" she asked impulsively.

His eyes narrowed. His face was a carved mask. "What are you trying to make me admit to, Glenda— or Gemma, if that's who you really are? That I proposed marriage to claim my nephew as my son and thereby give him the Ross name merely as a sop to my conscience? A noble falsehood, a fantasy, to cover the shabby reality that knowing you for the fickle tramp which you are, I still want you?"

"No . . . I didn't mean that at all."

"But you would have been right in thinking that. It's the demoralizing, unprincipled, barbarous truth. I want you, want you so much it's driving me out of my mind, beyond peace and self-respect into a black hell of hatred. I hate myself for wanting you; I hate you for being warm and responsive to me, for being able to switch brothers at the drop of a hat. For your heartlessness in thinking so little of Ian that you enjoy being touched by me. A decent woman wouldn't have let me come anywhere near her, yet it was as much as you could do to keep your hands off me. It would have needed only the slightest persuasion to make you mine. I could have got you into bed any time I wanted."

"It's a pity you didn't," she flung at him, incensed by his disbelief, his insistence even now that she was Glenda. "If you had got me into bed you wouldn't have had to take my word for it. You would have found out for yourself. Well, why don't you? The bed's there. What are you waiting for? Everything dealt with in one fell swoop, if you'll pardon the crudity."

"Why you . . ."

Disregarding the warning sparks in his eyes, she was past caring anyway, she continued with reckless abandon, refusing to mince words, "You could sate your passion and find an answer to the question that's burning you up—am I or aren't I the virgin I claim to be? And who knows—you might even give me the child you insist that I'm carrying."

"You're asking for it," he said thickly, his eyes dark and demented, his fingers traveling from her wrists to her upper arms, pulling her closer so that the full fury of his breath blasted across her cheek. "You're driving me to it. I won't be able to help myself; you don't need the usual trappings your sex is prone to resort to, a revealing dress, heady perfume. Your tongue is better than the deepest cleavage or the most evocative perfume."

She didn't know which she backed away from, the naked hunger in his eyes or his words. How was she to know that to him the compulsive step away would come under the heading of provocation and that he would be incensed enough to bring her back?

"You little torment. Never miss a trick, do you?" he said, this time drawing her fully into his arms, holding her so suffocatingly close that she couldn't breathe and then covering her mouth with a kiss which left no room for retreat and swept her into a vortex of feeling. It was like melting in a vat of pure sensation. Not just her burning lips, but her whole body was ultra-sensitized. She was electrically aware of his fingers sliding down her neck, easing away the material of her dress to give his lips access to her bared shoulder.

His kiss showered her flesh with delight and she brushed her fingers across his lowered cheek, realizing the truth in at least one accusation he'd made. She did want to touch him, incessantly and involuntarily. She hadn't realized there was anything wrong in that. It stemmed from her innocent desire to express the depth of her feelings through her fingers, and perhaps also to reassure herself that he was real and not a figment of her romantic heart. Her *foolish* heart, which bound her more securely than bars or chains. In her carefree, heartfree days she had hoped that love would come to her and had thought it would be a blessing. The realization had dawned on her slowly that it could also be a bondage, a sweet bondage when it was reciprocal and hearts were united, a bitter bondage when the love was not returned. The bitterness of Maxwell's desire was as far removed from love as it was possible to be. It made a mockery of her earlier belief that the marriage with the greatest chance of survival was the one where physical attraction sparked off love. She had even thought that when the attraction was strong enough love must inevitably follow.

She wasn't aware that her distress had found an outlet and that she was crying in self-pity at the hopelessness of her plight—because she could not find happiness with Maxwell like this, but neither could she find happiness without him—until he molded his fingers to her cheeks to dry her tears. He did this awkwardly, with none of his usual finesse, as if in all his dealings with women this was a new turn-up.

His voice was biting but not brutal, brusque but not bitter. "You've got to leave my room. We both need to cool off."

She didn't see Maxwell again until much later in the day and his attitude toward her was impersonal and even a little distant. There was no monitor on her movements and she supposed it would have been the simplest thing in the world to telephone for a taxi to take her to the station and catch the next train home. So easy in theory, so hard to do. She could no more walk out on Maxwell now than she could stop breathing. She couldn't leave him of her own free will. If he wanted her to go he would have to send her away. She hoped it wouldn't be until after Ian's funeral. She wanted to be by his side for that.

She phoned Barry again, this time without interruption. She couldn't have left him hanging, not knowing where she was or what was happening to her. Her earlier phone call, so abruptly ended when Maxwell took the receiver from her and banged it down to cut off the connection, would have worried him more than no phone call at all.

Barry came on the line and practically his first words were, "Give me your address and then if that lunatic, whoever he is, cuts us off again I'll know where to come to sort him out."

The idea of Barry sorting Maxwell out was so ludicrous that it took all her composure not to laugh. "That won't be necessary, Barry, but thank you all the same. When I phoned before I had . . . er . . . something like that in mind, but it isn't fair to put you to the trouble of coming all this way. I'm in Scotland, incidentally, and I'm in no danger. I really am all right. Will you go round and see Miss Davies and give her that message? Please do this for me. If you see her and talk to her she'll take it in much better than a phone call, which might panic her. Tell her I'm safe and that there's nothing to worry about and I'll get in touch with her myself later. Would you also pass that same message on to my neighbors, please? I hate to think that anyone's been distressed by my disappearance."

"Disappearance? What disappearance? What are you talking about? I was hurt that you didn't confide in me in advance, but no one's had any cause for distress. Concern, yes, because Miss Davies said your voice sounded different. Choked up like, but that was to be expected."

"Miss Davies said? I don't understand. When was this?"

"Really, Gemma! What's the matter with you? When you phoned her, of course, before you left, apologizing for the short notice and asking for time off. Something about a family crisis."

"That must have been Glenda. She seems to have thought of everything. I'm glad she made my excuses for me."

Glenda had certainly paid meticulous attention to detail. But whether she had made the phone call to Miss Davies to put everyone's mind at rest or because she knew that Gemma would start screaming to Maxwell that she was Gemma Coleridge was another matter entirely. If fears had not been allayed at that end there was always the possibility of her disappearance being reported in the newspapers and the danger of Maxwell spotting it. She wasn't going to have her plans spoiled by that and she had taken steps to eliminate the risk. Even if it was to suit her own purpose, Gemma was glad that Glenda had phoned Miss Davies and that she hadn't been a worry to anyone.

"What did you say about Glenda?" Barry queried sharply.

"Oh, nothing important. I read in the newspapers that she was missing. Has she turned up yet?"

"No. Her father's offering a fantastic reward for news of her whereabouts. Do you know anything about it, Gemma?"

"What could I know?" she countered.

"If you know where she is you should speak up."

"I honestly don't know where Glenda is," she replied truthfully.

"I'm still not satisfied. It sounds decidedly fishy to me, your going off like that and not letting on to me. I

didn't know you had any close family. I think you've
been pretty secretive all the way round."

"I'm sorry you're taking this attitude, Barry, and I'm
sorry that you feel I'm being secretive. If I am it can't
be helped. I can't say more now. This is a long-
distance call and I'm using someone else's phone."

"If it belongs to the lunatic who cut me off, to hell
with him. Let him pay."

"I can't do that. I must go."

"Give me your number, then, and I'll ring you back.
I think you know more than you're saying. There
could be rich pickings here, you know."

"I'm not interested in that angle. I don't know
anything that would help anyone to find Glenda. I
can't talk anymore just now."

"When you do want to talk I might not want to
listen," he said pettishly. "What kind of a future are
we going to have if there's no trust between us?"

"Oh, Barry, I'm so sorry. I didn't want to tell you
this over the phone, but we have no future together."

"What are you talking about? Of course we have!
Have you been stringing me along?"

"Barry, no! But I haven't been taking anything for
granted, either."

"Well I have. I took it for granted that one day we'd
get married."

"I'm sorry, Barry, but it's no good."

"Gemma . . . don't ring off."

"Goodbye, Barry," she said, gently setting the
receiver back in its cradle.

The day of Ian's funeral dawned. There was sleet in
the wind and a terrible forlornness, a bitter desolation
in her heart. She had never known Ian, but as she
stood by Maxwell's side on that bleak Scottish hillside
hot tears fell down her cold cheeks.

Long after they'd left the graveyard she could still hear the mournful music that had piped Ian to his last resting place. The melancholy of the occasion was especially poignant because Ian was so young. People kept approaching Maxwell to express sympathy, curiosity in their eyes as they glanced at the pale-faced girl standing by his side in the dark dress and coat which she had hastily purchased for the event. Among the throng of mourners were a number of relatives, aunts, uncles, and several cousins, as well as many friends. One person was noticeably absent.

"Glenda should have been here," Maxwell said, voicing the thought that had been spinning through Gemma's mind.

She couldn't believe her own ears. "Did I hear you right?"

His hand lifted to touch her cheek. "Yes . . . Gemma."

He had called her Gemma. It couldn't be left there, they both knew that, but now wasn't the moment for a personal discussion. Some of the mourners had traveled long distances and needed to be put up for the night. Morag required help to prepare the rooms and feed the sudden influx of guests. Even Fiona buckled in and the three of them, aided by Jeanie, the little maid who had shown Gemma to her room when she first came to Glenross, worked industriously to insure everyone's comfort. Gemma knew that it was an uneasy truce between her and Fiona. They were both rivals for Maxwell's affections and there could never be room for them under the same roof on a permanent basis.

The house seemed all the quieter when the guests departed. As soon as the door closed on the last straggler, Maxwell asked Gemma to come with him to his study . . . for a word.

But once there he took her hands in his and looked at her for a long time without speaking. Then all he said was, "Gemma."

"Yes?"

"Just Gemma."

Tears blurred her vision. She brushed them impatiently away, marveling at the tenderness that came to his eyes as he spoke her name, her real name at last. She had begun to think she must have dreamed that he'd commented on Glenda's absence and called her Gemma as they'd stood by Ian's grave.

"I've explained the situation to Fiona and Morag."

"What did they say?"

"Morag was bemused, but very delighted. Now Fiona—" he looked puzzled—"I thought she'd stay on to help you settle in . . . kind of ease you into the running of the house . . . but she thinks it's better if she goes. She's packing now. She said that you'd understand."

Yes, she understood. "What finally convinced you that I'm not Glenda?"

"I'd like to say that I came to my senses, but that would be a lie. I don't think I'll ever come to my senses where you're concerned. I went through hell imagining that you had belonged to someone else, that the evidence of the love you had given was in the child you bore. Ian had raved about you and I expected a looker, but when I saw you it was as if the whole world had suddenly shattered beneath my feet. I was that badly hit."

"Ian told you about Glenda, not about me," she corrected gently. "I never knew your brother."

"I realize that now. You would have been good for him as she never was, but I'm not unselfish enough to wish it had been you. I want you for myself. Even driven half crazy by all the things I thought about you,

I still wanted you." His mouth contorted in self-derision. "Heaven knows I'm no saint, and you weren't putting up very strong 'keep off' signals. In fact, you seemed to be offering yourself to me with every look and I don't know how I managed to stop myself from taking you up on it and ravishing you. I was sick with disgust that I could feel that way about you. I tried to tell myself that you were bad all the way through and knew every possible way to excite a man. I waited for the badness to show through. It always does. It isn't something that can be concealed for any length of time. But the reverse of what I expected happened. Every day you grew more angelic-looking and lovelier before my eyes, as if reflecting an inner purity. It just about drove me out of my mind. I was half-crazed with jealousy and eaten up with desire for you." He groaned. "What do I mean *was?* I still am."

"Jealous?" she said, no longer feeling the need to chain her hands at her sides and letting her fingers trespass freely over the agony furrowing his brow and tightening his cheek in bitterness. "There's no one to be jealous of," she said in some amazement, still bemused by his caring and not properly taking it in.

"No? What about Barry?" he said thickly. "I came into this room and heard you talking to him on the phone, beseeching him to come for you." His hand crushed hers, bringing it from his cheek to his lips.

With his kiss searing her palm, she said brokenly, "You forbade me ever to speak to him again. I have a confession to make. I disobeyed you and phoned him back. Not because I cared anything for him, but because it would have been too cruel to leave him wondering what was happening after the way you slammed the phone down on him. If you'd heard that conversation you would have known that you had no cause to be jealous. I assured him that I was all right and then I said goodbye. I'm sure he got the message that it was a final goodbye. I only wanted him to come up to Scotland to help convince you who I was. You still haven't told me what did."

"I received a letter from Glenda," he said grimly. "You can read it, but the gist of it is that she apologizes for the trouble she's caused you. She asks me to forgive her and hopes you'll understand she was so desperate that when she saw the opportunity to involve you she didn't hesitate. It was much as we've already worked out—she wanted to get away to make up her own mind about whether to have the child or not. Have you any idea where she went?"

"Yes," Gemma said in a bright flash of inspiration. "I didn't know until this moment and yet it's so obvious that I don't know why it didn't occur to me before. Who else would a girl go to if she was in trouble? Her parents are separated. Her mother lives in the south of France. That's where she went, wasn't it? To her mother."

"Yes. Reading between the lines, I gather that her parents didn't part amicably and that there's still a lot of bad feeling between them. All the time her father has been tearing his hair out and increasing the reward he offered for information and appealing for her to come home her mother had her in hiding."

"I presume her mother didn't try to influence her decision."

"Right."

"So?" But even as she was biting back her impatience to know she felt that she already knew the answer just by looking at his face.

"She lost the baby."

"Oh, no! How could she? I was so sure it would go

the other way once she got away from her father. How could she not want her own baby?"

"Don't upset yourself, darling," he said, looking deep into her troubled eyes, concerned, but pleased by her distress because it showed a depth of feeling that matched his own. She knew this by the tender little smile that eased the grimness of his mouth. "If the tone of her letter is anything to go by, I think you'll find Glenda a changed person. She decided to keep the baby. It wasn't to be."

"You mean she lost it naturally?"

"Yes, she miscarried."

"How dreadful for her. Poor Glenda. Does she know about Ian?"

"Not yet. Her letter arrived on the day of Ian's funeral. I shall have to go to France and see her. It's not something that can be put in a letter. I feel that I owe it to Ian's memory to break the news to her as gently as possible."

"I agree."

"She also had a change of heart about Ian. In her letter she says that as soon as she's well enough to travel she's coming back, to be with him."

"It's so distressing. It's a double loss for her."

"Second chances don't come often in this life. That's why I'm so grateful for mine. I'm not taking too much for granted, am I? You will give me another chance, won't you, my darling? My Gemma. Undeserving as I am, I beg you to let me prove my love for you."

"Your . . . ?" Had he said love?

"How I love you and want you!" he said with such burning passion and sincerity that her eyes flooded with tears again.

She couldn't believe it. It was so wonderful. She gazed up at him, making a gift of her devotion in the look of incredible joy on her face. "Say that again, please, Maxwell," she implored.

"I want you."

Her heart raced; her blood turned to fire and her body was like melting wax, desiring nothing more than to mold to his until their mutual hunger was satisfied. It was agonizing to hold herself in restraint and say huskily, "That's been obvious all along. I mean the other thing you said."

The tender smile played about his mouth again to tug at her heart. "Gemma, my sweet and lovely, adorable Gemma, I love you." The gentle truth in his eyes made it an act of reverence. "Don't make me wait too long, darling."

"I love you, Maxwell. I won't make you wait at all."

"Wanton," he reproved. "I see that I shall have to be strong-willed enough for both of us. Having managed to curb myself this far I'm sure I can hold on a while longer and take you pure to the altar."

"Spoilsport," she chided in mischievous retaliation.

He immediately made a grab for her and the love-talk temporarily ceased, save for the occasional groan and gasp of ecstasy as he proceeded to test his strong will to the limit. She didn't help matters by living up to the name he had called her. She was wanton in her love for him, wanton in her trust. She couldn't give her heart and keep her head. She shared greedily in the physical delights, but the moral aspect was all his, a responsibility that weighed heavily. She could tell this by the raggedness of his breathing, the devouring hunger of his kisses, which set her mouth on fire.

They kissed and touched, delighted and excited one another, murmuring incoherent endearments in between times. When her mouth was sated his lips moved downward, following the course his hands had taken, cherishing her breasts, tingling them and firing her imagination. If this was just the preliminary, what would the total act of lovemaking do to her? Her body was an explosion of feeling and her heart contained more love than she had thought possible.

"Darling," she whispered, her eyes worshiping the dear, rugged contours of his face. "I can hardly believe this is happening. I thought that once you found out that I wasn't Glenda you wouldn't want me anywhere near you and that you would send me away."

"Send you away?" Anguish momentarily shadowed his adoring eyes. "Don't torture me by even suggesting such a thing."

"I didn't want to go. I dreaded it. Don't laugh at me, will you? I was even crazy enough to wish that I was carrying a child that should rightfully bear the name of Ross just so you would have to marry me."

"Now you're tormenting me. Don't push your luck. I'd need very little persuasion to grant that wish."

"I hope you do . . . one day."

They looked at one another, each savoring the thought of his child growing in her body.

"On the subject of sending you away," he said at length, "I think I will have to . . . send you home. But only until we can organize a wedding and you can return as mistress of Glenross."

"Mistress of Glenross!" she said in awe. "That sounds very grand." Her eyes grew thoughtful for a moment, then danced with mischief again. "Until I am, couldn't I stay and be *your* mistress?"

He groaned. "Have you no pity? First torture, then torment, now temptation."

"And tomorrow?" she said, serious once more. "What will tomorrow bring?"

Into the hushed moment Maxwell's voice fell as

sincerely as a vow. "More happiness than I deserve or ever thought possible. A lifetime of happiness, my love."

His love, enslaving her heart. A lifetime of sweet bondage. She rested her cheek against his broad chest, supremely content.

Silhouette Desire

Now Available

Come Back, My Love by Pamela Wallace

TV newsperson Toni Lawrence was on the fast track to fame when photographer Theo Chakiris swept her off her feet at the Royal Wedding. Storybook romances belonged to princes and princesses! She tried to forget, to bury herself in her work, but passion brought them together to recapture the glory of ecstasy.

Blanket Of Stars by Lorraine Valley

Greece was the perfect setting for adventure and romance, and for Gena Fielding it became the land she would call home. In Alex Andreas' dark eyes she saw a passion and a glory, a flame to light the way to sensual pleasures and melt her resistance beneath the searing Greek sun.

Sweet Bondage by Dorothy Vernon

Maxwell Ross had set into motion a plan to avenge his younger brother. But he was wreaking revenge on the wrong woman, as Gemma Coleridge was only too happy to tell him—at first. But soon, too soon, her heart overrode her head. She lost her anger in Maxwell's arms, and dared to dream of a happiness that would last forever.

Silhouette Desire

Now Available

Dream Come True by Ann Major

Six years after their divorce, Barron Skymaster, superstar, tried to claim Amber again. But how could she face him after denying him knowledge of his own son—a son he had every right to know? Would that knowledge bring them together again or would it tear them apart forever?

Of Passion Born by Suzanne Simms

Professor Chelsie McBride was thoroughly acquainted with her subject—the sometimes humorous, sometimes bawdy Canterbury Tales. A respected professional in her field, she was no stranger to the earthy side of passion. But when it was introduced to her in the person of Drew Bradford, she realized she'd only been studying love by the book.

Second Harvest by Erin Ross

The fields of Kia Ora were all that remained of Alex's turbulent past, and Lindsay was bound to honour her husband's memory by taking an active part in the New Zealand vineyard. But what she began with reluctance soon became a fervent obsession. The exotic splendour of Kia Ora was captivating, and Philip Macek, its hard-driving owner, held her spellbound.

Silhouette Desire

Coming Next Month

Lover In Pursuit by Stephanie James

Reyna McKenzie vowed she'd never again succumb to Trevor Langdon's promise of love. But he'd come to Hawaii determined to reclaim her and under the tropical sun, she soon found herself willing to submit to the love she so desperately wanted.

King of Diamonds by Penny Allison

Carney Gallagher was baseball's golden boy, now in the troubled last season. Flame-haired Jo Ryan, the Atlanta *Star's* rookie woman sports reporter, made her first career hit at his expense. Gallagher vowed to even the score . . . but Jo never imagined that passion would be the weapon of his choice.

Love In The China Sea by Judith Baker

Kai Shanpei, mysterious Eurasian tycoon, was as much a part of Hong Kong as its crescent harbour, teeming streets and the jagged mountains looming above. From the moment she met him Anne Hunter was lost in his spell, plucked from reality and transported into his arms to learn the secrets of love.

Silhouette Desire

Coming Next Month

Bittersweet In Bern by Cheryl Durrant

Gabi Studer couldn't resist Peter Imhof's offer of
work in Switzerland, but she hadn't reckoned on
living in the same magnificent Alpine chalet as
the famed author. Alone together on the
enchanted Swiss mountainside, temptation was
only a kiss away.

Constant Stranger by Linda Sunshine

Murphy Roarke literally knocked Joanna
Davenport off her feet. She'd come to New York
to launch a publishing career, and Roarke had
helped her every step of the way . . . until he
stole her heart, demanding that she choose
between the job of a lifetime and a stormy,
perilous love.

Shared Moments by Mary Lynn Baxter

He was the devil in disguise. Kace McCord, the
silver-haired client Courtney Roberts tried to
keep at arm's length. But he took possession of
her from the first, arousing her feelings and
driving her to heights of rapture.

THE MORE SENSUAL
PROVOCATIVE ROMANCE

95p each

1 ☐ CORPORATE AFFAIR
Stephanie James

2 ☐ LOVE'S SILVER WEB
Nicole Monet

3 ☐ WISE FOLLY
Rita Clay

4 ☐ KISS AND TELL
Suzanne Carey

5 ☐ WHEN LAST WE LOVED
Judith Baker

6 ☐ A FRENCH-MAN'S KISS
Kathryn Mallory

7 ☐ NOT EVEN FOR LOVE
Erin St. Claire

8 ☐ MAKE NO PROMISES
Sherry Dee

9 ☐ MOMENT IN TIME
Suzanne Simms

10 ☐ WHENEVER I LOVE YOU
Alana Smith

11 ☐ VELVET TOUCH
Stephanie James

12 ☐ THE COWBOY AND THE LADY
Diana Palmer

13 ☐ COME BACK MY LOVE
Pamela Wallace

14 ☐ BLANKET OF STARS
Lorraine Valley

15 ☐ SWEET BONDAGE
Dorothy Vernon

16 ☐ DREAM COME TRUE
Ann Major

17 ☐ OF PASSION BORN
Suzanne Simms

18 ☐ SECOND HARVEST
Erin Ross

All these books are available at your local bookshop or newsagent, or can be ordered direct from the publisher. Just tick the titles you want and fill in the form below.

Prices and availability subject to change without notice.

SILHOUETTE BOOKS, P.O. Box 11, Falmouth, Cornwall.

Please send cheque or postal order, and allow the following for postage and packing:

U.K. – 45p for one book, plus 20p for the second book, and 14p for each additional book ordered up to a £1.63 maximum.

B.F.P.O. and EIRE – 45p for the first book, plus 20p for the second book, and 14p per copy for the next 7 books, 8p per book thereafter.

OTHER OVERSEAS CUSTOMERS – 75p for the first book, plus 21p per copy for each additional book.

Name ....

Address ....

....